The Mystery of the
EMPTY ROOM

By **AUGUSTA HUIELL SEAMAN**

Cover illustration by Sam Kweskin

SBS SCHOLASTIC BOOK SERVICES
New York Toronto London Auckland Sydney

Copyright 1953 by Augusta Huiell Seaman Freeman.

Illustration copyright 1949 by Pocket Books, Inc. This edition is published by Scholastic Book Services, a division of Scholastic Magazines, Inc., by arrangement with Doubleday & Company, Inc.

15th printing ....February 1970

Printed in the U.S.A.

CONTENTS

1. Herbertstown

IT DID NOT seem possible that there *could* be such a place as Herbertstown! At least not to Lois Shelton. Jean apparently didn't care, one way or another, and neither, as far as Lois could see, did Ellen McConkey. All three had just been rattled about for miles over a rutty, muddy, back-country road, in the most decrepit and ancient taxi they had ever seen. Jean had openly enjoyed the bumps, rocketing into the air and squealing with delight at every "thank-you-marm." But she *would* be liable to act that way, being but twelve and still capable of being entertained by such rough going! Ellen McConkey had kept her great bulk anchored down to the sagging seat, but grunted heavily at each jolt and held out a protecting arm on each side of her to keep her charges from tumbling to the floor of the ancient little Ford car. Lois, trying to maintain the dignity of her seventeen years, had sturdily refrained from any undue appearance of discomfort, and only murmured occasionally to Ellen, who was seated between the sisters, "*Can't* you keep Jean from making such a nuisance of herself, Ellen? She'll break the springs of this seat—if there are any left to break!"

Then they had turned a corner and driven into Herbertstown. None of them would have suspected it to be the goal of their long journey, except for the driver turning about and announcing:

"Here you are, ma'am. This here is Herbertstown. And now, whereabouts would you want me to put you down?"

They stared about them at the one not very long, unpaved

street, lined at intervals with ancient and rather weather-worn wooden houses sheltered by tall, melancholy trees, dismally creaking in the waning light of a November afternoon. Then they stared at one another in wordless dismay.

"We want to be put down at the house of Mr. Silas Trott," faltered Lois, hoping desperately that the aforesaid house would prove to be well outside of this dreary town, at least. The driver said he would get down and inquire at the one "general store," near which they had halted, as to the whereabouts of the house of Mr. Silas Trott. He came back in a moment to announce, "Can't miss it! Last house on the street, right-hand side, facin' the way we're headed." He got in and drove them to its gate, dumped them out on the roadside with all their baggage, without even offering to carry it in, accepted his fee from Ellen, and rattled away into the dusk, leaving them standing forlornly facing a closed door.

The house itself was of the typical New Jersey Colonial vintage, sadly in need of paint and repairs, but dignified and graceful in architecture, had they but had the time or the interest to take note of it. But they had neither. They saw only the long picket fence around the place—broken and in spots altogether missing—the rattling shutters, one or two hanging by a single hinge, the general appearance of neglect and disrepair everywhere apparent—and their hearts sank in deep misgivings. At least the heart of Lois did, and presumably that of Ellen McConkey. Jean, on the contrary, was fazed by nothing and took the whole affair as a wild lark.

Lois mounted the steps of the porch and thumped the ponderous knocker, and they all waited in a breathless pause. There was no response. Jean scrambled round to the back of the place to see whether there would be any better luck at a rear or side door. She came flying back to report, "Nothing doing! Everyone's out and the house is locked up!"

"Whatever shall we *do?*" quavered Lois. And Ellen McConkey muttered darkly something to the effect of "turnin' me poor little orphans out on the street!" and her private opinions of such conduct. Suddenly, from across the road, a voice piped up in the gathering dusk:

"You wanna buy some secondhand furniture? Mr. Trott, he went away this mornin' t' get another load. He'll be back pretty quick, but it'll be too dark to show you through the sheds!"

At this extraordinary announcement they all whirled about and beheld a small boy hanging over the fence of the house across the way. They could not see him very plainly in the dusk, but he looked to be about twelve or thirteen years old and was evidently devoured with curiosity about them.

"Who are you?" shouted Jean, always the first to rise to an emergency.

"I'm Sandy Coleman," he roared back. "I live here. If you want any furniture, guess you'll have to come tomorrow."

"We don't want any furniture," declared Lois with dignity. "I don't know what you mean. We've come here to stay with Mr. Trott. He's our guardian and he is expecting us. Where is he?" The small boy gaped open-mouthed at this information, dropped off the fence and sauntered over to the group.

"Gee!" he exploded. "Say, d'you really expect ter *live* here? Can you beat *that!* And with old Si Trott, in the bargain!"

"Ye'll keep a civil tongue in yer head, young man, while

yer talkin' to us," growled Ellen McConkey, suddenly rising to the occasion, "an' not be callin' Mr. Trott by his first name like that! Ye deserve a good shakin' by the collar!"

Sandy instantly perceived that he'd made a mistake. And like the little gentleman that at heart he was, he made his apology:

"Oh, heck! I didn't mean nuthin' by that. Old Si—I mean, Mr. Trott—is a dandy—he sure *is*! But we all call him 'Si' around here. He likes us to. He's awful good-natured!"

"Is he?" queried Jean. "Well, I'm glad to hear *that*. He was a friend of our family. We've been left in his care. We never saw him, though, so we didn't know just what he was like. Only he's sent for us to live with him here, 'cause Dad didn't leave very much money when he died and we didn't know what to do for a home, and—"

"That'll do, Jean," interrupted Lois rather crisply. "You don't have to tell all our family history to the first stranger you meet here." Jean subsided for a moment, somewhat squelched, but Sandy was in no way abashed.

"Oh, that's all right," he reassured them seriously. "I ain't tellin' no tales, and it won't go any further if you don't want it to. I'm kinder glad you've come myself, 'cause now I'll have someone to play with. Though I wish it had been another boy," he added with unconcerned candor. "There ain't so many kids around here."

"But I'm just as good as a boy," Jean informed him earnestly. "I can climb trees and play baseball and—"

But stout old Ellen McConkey, the two girls' nurse since they had both been babies, was growing very impatient, as well as very cold, and she now interrupted to demand:

"Well, where *is* this here Mr. Silas Trott, I'd like to know? He knowed we was a-comin' today 'cause Miss

Lois wrote him so. An' now he's gone off an' left the place and locked the door, leavin' us to freeze in the street. Nice doin's, I call it!"

"Well, he couldn't help it, I guess," Sandy proceeded to enlighten them. "Y'see, it's this way. Mr. Trott buys second-hand furniture. He's got sheds an' sheds of it out in the yard there an' all over the place. He goes an' buys it at auctions or wherever they're selling out a house or a farm. You'd be surprised at all the queer things he buys an' has around this place. I guess he heard of a sale somewheres unexpected, 'cause he went off early this morning. I saw him go."

"But what does he buy such a lot of that stuff *for?*" demanded Lois, puzzled to understand the situation.

"Why, then he sells it again—if anyone wants to buy it," Sandy informed her. "Every once in a while someone comes here an' buys somethin'. Only Si—I mean Mr. Trott —says the business never did pay him, an' he mostly does it 'cause it amuses him. Says he can't keep away from an auction sale or sellin' off a farm."

"Does he live here all alone?" demanded Ellen Mc-Conkey, looking the establishment over with great disfavor.

"All 'cept old Zeph, the colored man who helps him round the place an' drives the truck when they get furniture—Hi!—there they are now, comin' up the road!" The boy scrambled down from the old gate on which he had been swinging as he talked and added:

"Guess I better fade away 'bout now! I was teasin' Zeph this mornin' an' he don't like me any too much. Bye-bye, all! I'll be seein' you!" He loped across the road and disappeared around the back of his own house. The three newcomers continued to stand where they were as the truck wheeled into the yard and drew up before one of the long sheds. Several minutes later a tall, rather corpulent figure came lumbering around the corner of the house. And in the purple dusk of the early November evening, Mr. Silas Trott and his new charges had their first glimpse of one another.

"My, my, *my!* This is too bad!" exclaimed Mr. Trott over and over, when Lois had introduced herself and the others. "I never intended it to be like this. Have you all been waiting long? You must be very cold. I was called away unexpectedly on a sale, but thought I'd be back long before this. Thee wrote me thee'd be here about five, didn't thee, Lois?

"Well, well, *well!*" he continued to exclaim. "So thee is Lois and thee is Jean—and *thee* is good Ellen McConkey! I'm downright glad to welcome thee all. But come in, come right in. Thee'll find this a queer household, I expect, but I'll try to make thee all comfortable."

A light had appeared at the front windows—a great oil lamp carried in by Zeph, so the newcomers suspected. And Ellen McConkey's heart sank deeper, if anything, at the suspicion that there was no electricity in the house—probably in the whole town. Then Mr. Silas Trott unlocked the front door and ushered the trio into the strangest-looking establishment they had ever beheld or imagined!

2. Through Two Pairs of Eyes

IT was a very cold room—an immense room, which contained one spool-bed (late Colonial) and one huge canopied affair of an Italian type. Various other decrepit and semi-decrepit articles of furniture were scattered about —an enormous highboy (early Colonial) very much chipped and battered and minus one leg, which lack was supplied by a number of bricks. There was also an extraordinarily ugly washstand of mid-Victorian vintage, on which rested a washbasin and pitcher decorated with violent red and green flowers of no known species. What little warmth there seemed to be (and it wasn't much!) was supplied by an old-fashioned Franklin stove boasting three firm legs and a very unstable fourth. The stove had a tiny coal grate which produced a cheery and comforting appearance but singularly little real heat.

On one side of the stove, in a huge, carved Jacobean chair, sat a very miserable Lois, writing industriously in a fat notebook that had a green leather cover and a metal clasp which could be locked by a tiny key. On the other side of the stove, in a Boston rocker whose sagging seat upholstery was inadequately concealed by a faded sofa cushion, crouched Jean, very sleepy and also scribbling rapidly in a notebook similar to her sister's, except that its cover was red.

In the background hovered Ellen McConkey, grumbling and muttering as she unpacked a steamer trunk and two suitcases, putting their contents into the drawers of the highboy or hanging them on hooks behind a faded chintz curtain in a far corner.

"I'll be about done now," she announced at last, glancing at the two by the fire. "It's a strange sort of place for the two of ye, but mebbe by tomorrow I can make it more comfortable. Ye'll best both of ye be sleepin' in this double-decker here, for I'm thinkin' that diddlebat over there" (she pointed to the spool-bed) "will be fallin' to bits before mornin'. Now I'm off to me own cubbyhole, an' it's right down the hall here, in case ye're needin' me." Lois looked up and tried feebly to smile.

"Thanks, Ellen, and good-night!" she said. "Don't worry about us. We'll be turning in soon, too. I hope you'll be comfortable."

"As comfortable as a soul could be in a bed with two straw mattresses and a feather one atop of it all. But I'm that sleepy I could lay me down on the floor this minute and drop off. Ye'd best be done with yer writin' and turn in," Ellen ended anxiously.

"We will—as soon as we've finished with our diaries," Lois assured her. And Ellen betook herself to her own quarters.

The matter of the diaries was a very important one to the girls because it concerned their dead father, whom both of them adored. On the first of that year he had presented them with the two fat little journals, and, in a talk they were never to forget, he had begged them to start the habit of keeping one each year, beginning thus early in their lives, and writing in them as frequently as possible.

"It is a matter of great regret to me," he had told them, "that no one saw to it that I started this habit in my early years. I've kept one religiously for the last twenty, and the diaries are a constant pleasure to me to refer back to. I'd give almost anything I possess, though, if I'd had them for my youth and young manhood too. Life is a deeply interesting affair always, no matter what one's circumstances are, and it's a pity not to record the golden moments, and the hard ones as well, for you'd be surprised how much you forget—how inaccurate your memory of former events can be—when you come to your later years. So promise me you will both at least *try* to keep some record of your youth, beginning now. And maybe in after years you will do it as a matter of course."

They had promised him and for months had struggled, sometimes a bit rebelliously, to keep their fat little diaries written up to date. Then had come the black day when their adored father had suddenly been taken from them. And after that, remembering their promise, they had stuck to the task of writing in those diaries as an almost sacred duty, because it was something they could do to carry out his wishes. If one could have slipped behind Lois's chair at this moment and glanced over her shoulder, one might have found her record of the day something like this:

"We had the most awful shock when Uncle Si (that's what he's asked us to call him) opened the front door and we walked into this house! Nobody ever saw such a conglomeration of old furniture all crowded together in the hall and every room, and hundreds of dishes and glassware huddled on a big table in what was probably intended to be the dining room. They were even all over the floors too, so that you could hardly make your way around anywhere without stepping on something breakable. One room—I suppose Uncle Si would call it the living room—was a little clearer and more in order than the others. But even that had a dozen different kinds of clocks on the walls and mantel besides two grandfather's clocks

standing in the corners. I never dreamed of such a nightmare clutter of old furniture!

"I thought Ellen would have a fit, and I was deathly
scared for fear she would say something awful and hurt
Uncle Si's feelings. He is so nice and tries to be so kind
to us that I couldn't bear to have him feel hurt by what
we thought of his house. But fortunately Ellen kept her
opinions to herself, and he showed us upstairs to our rooms.
There were even old rugs, and bed quilts and draperies hanging over the stair railings, and it was hard to go up without brushing them down. Uncle Si remarked that he'd
have to clear up some of this mess, but he hadn't quite
had time yet. He said:

'Old Zeph and I have been fixing up a room or two for
thee and Jean and Ellen McConkey, and we picked out the
best furniture we could find. But I expect thee will want
to make some changes later. When you all are ready, come
down and have supper. Zeph is getting it ready now.'

"This room is terribly, terribly dreary. When I think of
our lovely little home in Upton, it doesn't seem possible
we could be reduced to this. I just don't dare let my thoughts
go back to my beautiful little white-and-green-chintz room
with the lovely little reading lamp on my desk. There is a
terrible, bad-smelling kerosene lamp on the table beside
me here—the only light in this great room. I mustn't,
mustn't think about it!

"When we went down to supper we found Ellen and
Zeph, who helps here, having a wrangle about who should
be in the kitchen and serve the meal and who should wait
on the table. Zeph declared he had always done both and
was going to do it now. Ellen announced that she wasn't
going to stand around idle and would much prefer to be
in the kitchen than wait on the table. Uncle Si settled it

by telling Zeph he was a better waiter than a cook and that Ellen could take over that job if she chose. Zeph didn't look too pleased. He's a thin, shrimp-like little person and used to having his own way a good deal, I imagine. I'm afraid he and Ellen aren't going to get on any too well.

"It was a queer sort of supper—cold ham and boiled rice and bread and butter, and—oh, horrors— *stewed prunes* for dessert. I hope Ellen *does* take over the cooking. She's a peach at that, and we won't have any more such meals as this one. We left the two of them to clear up afterward and went to sit with Uncle Si by his great red-hot stove in the living room—the only really warm and cozy place in the house. We talked a couple of hours about Daddy and all that had happened lately. At least Uncle Si and I talked, but Jean, after squirming around restlessly for a while, mysteriously disappeared and wasn't seen again till it was time to go to bed. Then I heard Ellen having an argument with her out on the porch, where Ellen found her shouting good-night to the small boy across the street.

"It seems Jean had got tired of our conversation and gone outside with her flashlight to look about the place— she's the greatest child for snooping into everything!— and had there discovered the boy again, hanging over his fence and staring at this house. They had made a voyage of discovery all about the yard and barns where Uncle Si stores his furniture—which expedition had abruptly ended when the boy's mother had called him home to go to bed. Jean declares that this 'Sandy' is a 'good sport' and that she's going to have a lot of fun playing with him. I hope she doesn't lead him into any mischief, for she's a young terror, if ever there was one! She had a very mysterious air when we came up to bed, and she informed me: 'I know something you don't know!' but refused to explain any further. I'm too tired to care what she knows, and I said so.

"Uncle Si is sweet to us. He said, when we bade him good-night. 'I hope you will both be happy in this house. I shall do my utmost to make you so.' But, oh, Daddy, Daddy—I miss you more terribly than ever tonight!"

Lois looked up from her journal at this point and saw that Jean, on the other side of the Franklin stove, had fallen asleep, her head on her arm, and her diary was slipping to the floor. Mechanically she rescued it and put it on the table beside the lamp. She did not look in it, for she had no particular interest in what her young sister had written, and besides, they had an unspoken compact that their journals were strictly private and personal and not to be seen by anyone else, unless by special invitation. But if she had opened it, she would have found the entry as follows:

"This is a grand house. I'm going to have a lot of fun in it. It's different from any house I ever lived in. Lois hates it and so does Ellen, but I like it. I'm not so fussy about always being comfortable and having things just so, as they are.

"Uncle Si is swell. He doesn't fuss all the time about what you do and how you behave. I like the way he calls us 'thee.' He says I must go to school. I don't think I'll like that except that Sandy goes to one here. Sandy says he thinks I'll be in his class.

"Sandy is a good egg. He was outside tonight when I went out to snoop around, hanging over his fence and gaping at this house. He said, 'Let's go look around the place,' so I had my flashlight and we went all around the big yard with the sheds where the furniture is stored. When the sheds get too full, Sandy says Uncle Si turns out the pieces he doesn't like or are more gone to bits and leaves them in the yard. There were the funniest things standing about in the yard—old chairs and tables and trunks and couches and even dishes and jugs and broken vases—right out in the rain and sun and all. I never heard of such a place. I'm going to have the grandest time exploring it in daylight!

"We couldn't see inside the sheds, for they were all locked up and the windows are too high to look through, but I'm going to ask Uncle Si to let me look through them tomorrow. I think there must be a secret or a mystery or something about this house. 'Cause Sandy said did I see those shutters at two windows on the second floor 'way at the end. They were shut tight, but all the other shutters were open. He said he thinks that's a secret room, because Uncle Si always keeps it locked and never lets anyone go in there—not even Zeph. He says no one knows what's in that room. Even the shutters to the windows are tight shut and you can't get 'em open from the outside. They're heavy wooden shutters and you can't see through them. He said he climbed up there once when Uncle Si was away and tried to get 'em open but it was no use. And his mother caught him and gave him a *paddling*—that's what he called it!

"This is certainly the grandest thing—to be living in a house with a *secret*—" And at this point, sleep must have overtaken the writer.

Lois woke Jean up and told her to get ready for bed, advising her to share the great canopied one with herself for that night. But Jean was determined to sleep in "the corkscrew one," as she had dubbed the spool-bed, and she leaped into it when she was ready as if she were diving into a pool. But Ellen's prediction was all too accurate, and Jean and the spool-bed crashed to the floor in a collapsed heap. Ellen came hurrying in at the appalling sound, and even Uncle Si called up from downstairs to know what was amiss.

It was a rather subdued and penitent Jean who finally crept in beside Lois in the great canopied "double-decker" and dropped off almost immediately into dreamless slumber.

3. Ellen McConkey's Point of View

IN THE late afternoon of the ensuing day, Ellen McConkey stood in the kitchen doorway and surveyed the scene in the side yard with great and unconcealed disapproval. Never, in all her forty years of service (and she had come from Ireland to this country, a girl of eighteen), had she beheld such a state of affairs as reigned in this singular household. Thirty of those years of service had been spent with the Shelton family in Massachusetts. She had come to them first as a housemaid in the home of the girls' grandparents, where she had remained twelve years, and when their only son was married, she had gone into his home to take charge of the household for the younger couple. She had served them faithfully in many capacities and had mothered the two girls when their own mother had been taken from them while Jean was still a small baby. Later the grandparents went, and, last of all, Mr. Shelton himself, with appalling unexpectedness, leaving the two girls without a near relative in the world, and very nearly penniless as well.

Lois had mournfully told her, shortly after Mr. Shelton's death, that they could no longer afford to keep her as there was no money and they were to go to an old friend of the family in New Jersey for a home. But Ellen had firmly refused to relinquish her care of them. She declared that she had saved up enough in former years to see her comfortably through a great many to come, and she was too old to be changing about and getting used to other people's ways. If Mr. Trott would allow her to come with the girls, she would be willing to make herself useful in any capacity in the new household. Truth to tell, Ellen adored her young charges, and life would have been insupportable to her away from them.

But when she had said she couldn't get used to other people's ways, she had not reckoned on the household of Mr. Silas Trott! The ways of this particular establishment were such as she had never dreamed of in her wildest imaginings. She had been prepared to cope with the peculiarities of a household run by a man, but the eccentricities of this place were something akin to a horrid nightmare.

Take breakfast, for instance! She had come down early from an uneasy night on her straw mattress, while her charges were still asleep, to see if she could find the wherewithal in the pantry to get up a palatable breakfast.

She had found "that little shrimp of a man" (so she mentally labeled Zeph) messing about with some none-too-clean pots and pans, and the smell of burning oatmeal and frying eggs was being wafted all through the rooms on the lower floor. A violent altercation had ensued, ending victoriously for Ellen, when she threw out the burning oatmeal and soggy eggs, washed and scoured the utensils, and began on a fresh supply of food. Zeph had slunk out to the side yard to pour his complaints into the ear of Silas Trott, who was beginning to unload and store away the miscellaneous junk they had brought in the night before. Ellen had heard him remark to the outraged man:

"Thee has met thy match at last, Zeph! Cooking never was thy strong point. Better let Ellen have a try at it and give me a hand with this stuff." Silas Trott had chuckled, knowing well that old Zeph would far rather mess about with his ineffectual cooking than help with the heftier job of moving furniture!

And Ellen had served a delicious, well-cooked breakfast with what supplies she had found available—a breakfast that Mr. Silas Trott was quick to appreciate, making a mental note that Ellen might be an asset to the establishment, after all.

But this victory had been Ellen's only triumph during the day. Other changes she had proposed to make had not met with favorable response from Mr. Trott, who had been long years settled in this peculiar mode of life and did not fancy having it disrupted.

"No, Ellen, thee must not disturb anything in the dining room at present," he had warned her, when she had proposed to clear out all the miscellaneous "junk" on the table and floor and restore the room to the purpose for which it had originally been intended. "Thee can expend all that energy on the rooms thee and the two girls occupy. I do not care how thee arranges them. But this part of my household arrangements must not be touched. Zeph and I tried to fix those rooms as best we could the other day, and I realize they may not be all they should be. Thee can choose any other articles of furniture thee wishes from my stock in the sales room outside, provided thee asks me first about them. But do not try to alter anything downstairs here."

"Well, may I dust them then, sir?" asked Ellen, somewhat humbled. "The dust is that thick over everything— beggin' your pardon!—that you dassent touch it with a fingertip without gettin' smutted." Mr. Silas Trott had laughed—a deep and rumbling laugh.

"Dust and wash anything thee likes, Ellen, but I fear thee'll find it a bigger task than thee bargained for!" he had assured her, as he turned back to the yard and the unloading of the wagon.

So Ellen had been forced to content herself with a thorough overhauling of the rooms she and the two girls occupied, and it had certainly taken her the greater part of the day. Lois had not been of any help to her. She had been listless and inert since her waking that morning, very depressed, and had done little save stroll about a bit after breakfast and then sit staring out of the window or pretending to read during all the remainder of the day. Ellen mentally made a note that the girl probably needed a tonic, and promised herself she would get some cod-liver oil at the first opportunity.

But Jean, now—that was another matter! Jean had been in the wildest spirits all day. Dashing upstairs and down, indoors and out, exploring every available nook and corner, Jean had outdone herself in offering to help, getting in the way, falling into things and over things, discovering all manner of useless and inappropriate articles to put in their rooms, and generally making a nuisance of herself.

On the pretext of choosing more attractive furniture for their rooms, Ellen and Jean lured Lois out to look through the sheds, which Mr. Trott had unlocked while he and Zeph unloaded their latest acquisitions in the way of secondhand furnishings. The main shed was an enormous affair, crowded with every variety of household articles in every stage of repair or disrepair. There were hundreds of nondescript or mid-Victorian pieces, lamps, china, and glassware, some imitation or real antiques in various stages of dilapidation, and a few very genuine pieces of real beauty, though sadly in need of refinishing and polish.

The floors were littered with cast-off books, scattered among stacks of pictures, ranging from faded photographs and highly colored chromos and prints to oil paintings. The sheer mass and accumulation of it all was bewildering to Lois and Ellen. But Jean ran about, frantic with excitement, climbing over heaps of furniture to examine articles stored in the rear, getting in the way of Silas Trott and Zeph, calling to Lois and Ellen to come and look at this or that, and generally complicating affairs.

Finally Mr. Trott had to restrain her with:

"There, there, *there,* Jean! Thee is getting too excited and delaying us with the work. Help Lois and Ellen to select the furniture thee wants for the rooms. Thee can see all the rest of this some other time."

It was singular how a word from Uncle Si, gently administered, could take all the wind out of Jean's sails and reduce her to humble obedience, when Lois and Ellen had wrestled in vain with the situation.

"All right, Uncle Si," she had capitulated. "I'll go and look around to see what I'd like. Can we have anything we want?"

"Anything within reason!" he had chuckled. "Though, if it's an antique piece and someone should want to buy it sometime, I might have to sell it and thee could replace it with another."

She had joined Ellen and Lois, and they had all three

walked about slowly, trying to decide what would make
their bedroom look more habitable. The trouble was that
any particularly attractive piece usually had something the
matter with it. A really lovely little mahogany vanity table
caught the eye of Lois. But its mirror was hopelessly
cracked and splintered. A deep, cozy-looking rocking chair
that had captured Ellen's fancy was found to be minus a
rocker. And a big, presentable Axminster rug, of a rich
blue and tan, had a great inkstain directly in the center of
it.

At last, however, they had decided on two small maple
beds of Colonial design with pineapple posts, a little maple
bedside table to stand between them, a larger table and
Queen Anne mirror to serve as a dressing stand, two com-
modious bureaus, and a few of the smaller rugs to scatter
about, besides a number of comfortable chairs, a bookcase,
and a couch to place by the windows. None of these was
entirely whole or in perfect condition, but Ellen had promised to do what she could toward polishing and mending.
And the very prospect of having something tangible to do
had cheered up Lois immensely.

Long before they had finished their selection, however
they had missed Jean. She had apparently vanished from
the scenes, and they gave her no further thought. Suddenly
they were all startled beyond words to hear the notes
of Schubert's "Marche Militaire" echo thrillingly through
the great, barnlike enclosure. Simultaneously they had all
caught their breath and looked questioningly about.

Over in a corner, back against the wall, behind a veritable
mountain of piled-up bureaus and sideboards, stood a very
old and battered grand piano. Its case was scratched and
marred, and one or two of the keys were minus their ivory
finish. But it was of a famous make, and its tones were still

true and resonant. The indefatigable Jean had spied it, clambered over the intervening mountain of furniture to get at it, and her music-loving fingers were wringing from it some of the strains she had been taught. And for her age, Jean played exceedingly well.

Everyone in the shed stood stock-still, gazing questioningly at one another and at Jean. In another moment the girl's flying fingers had changed to a different melody— the Chopin "Minute Waltz." It was in this instant that Ellen happened to be staring at Silas Trott, and she beheld a curious change come over the cheerful and smiling face of the old Quaker. His jaw set, his face stiffened, and his eyes seemed filled with pain. It was only instantaneous, and a moment later he was his usual self, but Ellen had been startled at the curious incident.

As abruptly as she had begun to play, Jean stopped, in the middle of a note, as it were, left the piano, scrambled over the furniture, and rushed over to Silas Trott, almost hurling herself at him and clasping his arm with her two hands.

"Oh, Uncle Si," she panted, "do, *do* let us have this old grand piano in the house! I *love* to play on it, and I know Lois will too. She plays much better than I do. We both love music, and we've studied it so long—and practiced it so much. We miss it dreadfully when we don't. Do say we can have it. We'll take it up in our room if you don't want it downstairs. Oh, *do* let us have it!"

For a moment Silas Trott looked bewildered and unhappy. Ellen was sure he was going to refuse. Lois looked eagerly at him, as if imploring him to agree, but she said no word. It was evident that a struggle was going on within him. Finally he said:

"Thee does not want that great big old instrument in thy room, Jean, and it would be difficult to get it there.

And there is no place for it downstairs. No, I think thee must leave it where it is. I have had several offers to buy it. But do not be disappointed. I have in a shed, at the other end of the yard, a very good, small upright piano that thee could have taken upstairs, I think, without too much trouble. That should give you both just as much pleasure. I have no judgment and no understanding of music myself. We Quakers were brought up in an earlier day entirely without it. But if it will give thee pleasure, thee can have that other piano as soon as I can arrange for two strong men to come and move it."

When he came to the end of this speech, to his utmost astonishment Jean threw both arms about him and gave him a tremendous hug. And Ellen saw his face suddenly beam with an expression of tenderness that made her like him better than she had thought would be possible an hour before. But she still wondered what had been the meaning of that expression of pain when Jean had played on the old grand piano.

All these scenes of the day ran through Ellen's mind like a panorama, as she stood in the kitchen doorway that late afternoon and grimly surveyed the amazing collection of miscellaneous junk that strewed the yard. "I'll be clearin' this up some day—if I have me way! But I'd better go slow about it for a while yet," she had promised herself. She had won her first struggle about taking charge of the meals, and had produced (after some shopping in the village general store) the most appetizing dinner that Silas Trott could remember having eaten in many moons. Her position in that respect was secure, and Zeph had been banished from the kitchen to other duties. But as to general clearing up and straightening out of that unparalleled muddle, Mr. Trott would not as yet hear of it.

"He's a quare man," muttered Ellen to herself. "He's got somethin' in his life back of all this, but he's not tellin' the story to anyone!" At this moment Lois joined her. The girl had been reading, up in her room, but had restlessly come down to look about again. She too surveyed the cluttered yard through puzzled and disapproving eyes and remarked to Ellen:

"It's *awful,* isn't it! But if Uncle Si is going to let us have that piano upstairs, and we can fix up the room nicely, perhaps I won't mind this so much."

While she was speaking, they both caught a glimpse of Jean slyly tiptoeing around a corner of the house and glancing behind her, as if watching something out of their sight. When she saw them she ducked back again and was lost to view. Nor did she reappear.

"That child is up to something, mark my word!" commented Ellen darkly. "There's mischief afoot!"

4. From the Journal of Lois

"WE HAVE been here just a week, but many things seem so very different from what they were when we first arrived. I thought, that first night, that I should never, *never* get used to it if I lived here a hundred years. Now everything is beginning to settle down and seem familiar, even the terrible clutter of old furniture and truck. And Uncle Si has been kindness itself to us. I know it must be a trial to him in some ways to have us here and have his usual mode of life rather upset. Yet he never allows us to see that it troubles him. Even when Ellen and Zeph squabble—as they are almost always doing!—he seldom appears to notice it. And he seems to be growing very fond of Jean and myself.

"We have the room fixed now—our own—so that it is really quite attractive. Ellen scrubbed and cleaned it till it was sanitary enough for a hospital! Then we did what we could to paint and polish and renovate the old furniture Uncle Si had let us select, and Ellen found some old curtains which looked quite nice after they were washed and ironed. So the room is very cozy now and a great pleasure to me to retreat into when I get too disgusted with things outside it.

"But the best of all is the piano—an upright one, and in not too poor condition, thought it needs tuning. It has a good tone, and Jean and I practice on it continually. I can forget everything when I start working on my music again. I have noticed one queer thing, though. When either of us begins to play on it, Uncle Si (if he is in the house) generally makes some excuse to get out and go away out of hearing. I can't think whether it's because he hates all music so much, or whether it's just something about piano music that annoys him. I have a feeling that it isn't that he hates *music* in general, because several times I have happened to catch him whistling away very musically, when he thought he was alone. He always stops instantly if anyone appears on the scene. It's rather a mystery—especially the way he acted about that old grand piano on the first day. Jean told me yesterday that she'd been in the shed that morning again, while Uncle Si and Zeph were moving in some more furniture, and she went to look again at the old grand piano—and *it was gone!* She asked Uncle

Si if it had been sold, and he merely remarked that it had been taken away. Jean said he acted as if he didn't want to talk about it, so she had the sense to drop the subject.

"I don't understand this 'old-furniture business' that Uncle Si carries on at all. I can't see why he goes on buying more and more secondhand stuff when he has already enough on hand to stock a dozen ordinary stores. And such utterly useless stuff as some of it is! The queerest lot of people come in, off and on, to look his stock over and sometimes buy. Jean, who sees a great many things around here that I don't, says that yesterday two old ladies from 'back country' somewhere came in and looked over literally everything he has in the place. But all they bought were some dreadful old feather pillows and a few used muffin tins. On the other hand, some nice-looking people in a handsome car drove up soon after and paid quite a lot of money for a mahogany Queen Anne mirror and two vases of old Jersey glass. And so it goes!

"Jean has begun to go to school—and hates it as usual. But she says it's better than being cooped up in boarding school, as she had been for the last year before we left Upton. She is in the same class with Sandy Coleman, across the street, and I imagine the two of them are raising 'particular Cain' a good deal of the time. I'm sorry for any teacher who has to 'wrastle' with Jean!

"Zeph and Ellen have at last settled their quarrel about affairs in the kitchen. Zeph has completely abdicated there and left the whole of that department to Ellen, much to the relief of us all. She takes entire charge of the meals, and we are having once more the nice ones that she always gave us. Uncle Si particularly appreciates it and says Ellen is the best cook he ever knew—which makes her absolutely *beam!* Zeph also appreciates it, I think, though he wouldn't give her the satisfaction of saying so for the world. Zeph resents having to do so much more work outside, and mutters darkly about his 'pore old back!' and blames it on all of us. He threatens to leave about every other day, but Uncle Si only laughs and says wild horses couldn't drag him away, really.

"But now I come to the thing that has been puzzling me since the very first day we got here—or, at least, the next morning. There is certainly some curious mystery about this house and about Uncle Si. One of the rooms on this floor is *locked*, tightly, and no one ever goes in or out of it unless it is Uncle Si, and he must do so when we are never around. I notice too that the windows of it, on the outside, are tightly shuttered and these shutters never seem to be opened. But the queer thing about it is that last night I happened to wake up—it must have been between two and three in the morning—and heard a sound in the hall, as if someone were stepping about rather softly. I thought it might be Ellen. I didn't see who else it could be, for Uncle Si's room is downstairs and Zeph sleeps out in one of the sheds that has been fixed up for him.

"Thinking Ellen might have been taken ill, I got up and opened our door just a crack and peeped out. To my astonishment, it was Uncle Si, still dressed as if he hadn't been to bed! And he was just unlocking the door of that closed room. While I watched, he slipped in and shut the door after him. I didn't like to seem to be spying on him, so I closed our door and went back to bed. But I couldn't sleep, and after a long time I heard him come out again, lock the door, and go downstairs. But it all seems very, very mysterious. Why should he keep a room like that locked and go to it only after he thinks everyone is asleep? I wish I dared ask him, but of course that's out of the question. I am *not* going to say a word to Jean about this, for she'd immediately begin a campaign to find out all about it. 'Let sleeping dogs lie!' is my motto with her!

"I miss the music lessons dreadfully, but am trying to do the best I can by myself and not get out of practice. I make Jean keep up her practicing too. Just now I'm polishing up on Chopin, particularly the 'Revolutionary Etude.' I hope it isn't all very annoying to Uncle Si. Jean is fast asleep long ago, and I ought to be too, so I must stop writing for this time."

5. Two New Faces

THE HAZY, golden sunlight of a warm, Indian summer morning lay on the single little main street of Herbertstown. Lois felt that it resembled very closely some of the tiny South Carolina towns she had once visited with her father. The same brooding air of serenity and quiet, not a soul in sight, the old houses dreaming peacefully behind the tall trees, halfway down the street the little white church spire pointing aloft, the "general store and post office" opposite it, with only a single ancient horse and buggy hitched outside. From the general appearance of Herbertstown, one might be still living in the middle of the last century.

Lois sat on the front steps of the porch and idly surveyed it all, filled with a pleasant, temporary content. Jean was safe in school, Ellen was deeply absorbed in the kitchen,

d Uncle Si and Zeph had driven off with the truck early
at morning to attend another "auction" in some distant
wn. There seemed nothing to disturb her, and she felt
e need of a long, uninterrupted interval to "think things
it." For underneath this temporary calmness and se-
nity Lois was, in truth, a seething furnace of unrest and
ncertainty. She was young and strong and active. She had
cently graduated from a well-known New England board-
g school and had hoped to go to college later. But her
ther's death and their ensuing loss of all income had put
i end to that hope. Uncle Si's generosity had relieved them
om present dilemma, but that did not solve the problem
f what she was going to do with her life and what Jean
as going to do with *hers*, later. They could not forever
resume on his hospitality and generosity.

Before she had arrived in Herbertstown, she had had
isions of possibly giving music lessons to the children in
ie place and making a small beginning that way. But *then*
he hadn't known Herbertstown! There were so few chil-
ren in the tiny village that it did not now even boast a
chool. A bus came for the handful of youngsters and took
hem to a larger town several miles away for their education.
ind the few children who actually did claim a residence
i Herbertstown had no idea of pursuing a musical career.
he could not imagine herself giving piano lessons, for in-
tance, to Sandy Coleman!

No, it must be something else. But what could it be?
Vhat else was she fitted for? She rested her elbows on her
nees and dug her fingertips into her cheeks in the intensi-
y of her concentration. So absorbed was she in the consid-
ration of this problem that she did not even notice a
ather handsome car that turned a corner and drove noise-
essly down the drowsy street and stopped directly in front

of the house. Nor did she sense that a quietly but expensively dressed woman had descended from it and had entered the gate, till the newcomer was directly beside her. Then, suddenly, she looked up. The woman was staring at her with a concentration of attention that was fairly startling.

"Oh, I'm sorry!" exclaimed Lois, coming to a halt in her meditations and leaping to her feet. "Is—is there anything you wish?"

"Yes—good-morning!" said the stranger. "I'm sorry I disturbed you. But can you tell me if I can see some of the furniture and other things I understand are for sale here?"

"It's too bad you came just today," answered Lois politely, "because Mr. Trott, who owns this place, is away—for the whole day—and everything is locked up. You see, he only shows these things himself."

The woman's face assumed a crestfallen expression.

"That *is* certainly too bad!" sighed the visitor. "Particularly as I've driven all the way over here from Philadelphia to see him and look over his stock." She seemed to hesitate, then suddenly brightened and exclaimed, "But perhaps you can help me out. By the way, I don't think I've ever seen you here before. I come over fairly frequently to see if Mr. Trott has anything new or interesting to show me. I thought he lived here alone."

"My sister and I have come to live with him," Lois informed her. "He is an old friend of the family." For some reason that Lois could not fathom, this information seemed to startle the stranger, though she strove very hard to hide it. She said:

"So that is it! Well, I daresay you can do something to help me out. I have come a long way, and I hate to go back disappointed, because I may not be able to get here soon

again. There are one or two things—of an antique nature—
that I'd like very much to see if Mr. Trott has acquired recently. Could you not show me round the place? Perhaps
I can make a selection even if he isn't here."

But Lois shook her head. Silas Trott had left very definite
orders for just such contingencies as this. "Thee must never
allow anyone to go through the sheds or into the house
while I am away," he had warned her at the very beginning.
"I do not wish it. People—unscrupulous ones—have sometimes taken advantage of my absence in the past to try to
get by Zeph and prowl around by themselves—and there are
many valuable things here that no one understands about
but myself. I shall leave the keys here, because in case of fire
or accident it might be necessary in my absence to open the
sheds. But thee must, on no account, allow any stranger to
enter them." So that was that!

"I'm *so* sorry!" apologized Lois, therefore. "But you see
I know nothing about the prices. Only Mr. Trott can tell
you that, so it wouldn't be any use, anyway." But the woman
was persistent.

"That wouldn't matter," she cried, "if only I can see what
I want. I could ask to have it reserved for me and come back
later and settle with Mr. Trott about the price—or write."

It sounded reasonable enough, but Lois was adamant,
and finally managed to convince the visitor that it was useless. With an impatient shrug and a brief good-morning,
the woman turned to go down the steps of the porch, when
suddenly Lois saw her stumble, turn, and half roll down
the shallow steps to the ground. Concerned lest she had in-
jured herself, Lois rushed to help her get to her feet. The
woman put her hand over her eyes and staggered a bit.

"Oh—I'm hurt!" she moaned softly. "I think I've twisted

my ankle. Could I—could I sit down somewhere—just a moment—and have a drink of water?"

"Of course—oh, I'm so sorry!" murmured Lois. "Let me help you into the living room and I'll get you a drink. You'd better sit quietly there till your ankle gets better." She assisted the woman up the steps and into the living room, calling to Ellen as they entered the house.

Ellen came hurrying from the kitchen, astounded at what she beheld, and Lois explained briefly what had happened. While Ellen went back for a glass of water, Lois suggested that they look at the ankle to see if it was swelling or needed some attention.

"No—no!" exclaimed the stranger, a bit impatiently, Lois thought. "I've only wrenched it a little. Just a few moments' rest is all it needs." While she spoke, her eyes were darting about the place, taking in every detail of the rather crowded and cluttered room. When Ellen returned, she drank a few sips of the water and handed back the glass. And all the while her darting eyes never rested. At length she tried her foot, stood on it and apparently found that she could use it without difficulty. It was then that her manner suddenly changed. Turning to Lois, she remarked gaily:

"Well, now that I'm in here, why not show me a few of these interesting things before I go? I'm certain Mr. Trott would not mind my looking around. I've seen the things in here while I've been sitting and gazing about. Is there anything else interesting in the other room across the hall—or upstairs?" Without waiting for consent, she got up, and limping slightly, started for the door that led to the hallway. Terribly perplexed as to what she ought to do or say, Lois followed close behind, sure now that there was something wrong about this persistent would-be customer. No genuine lady, she felt, would have taken advantage of her kindness and hospitality in this way. Yet she felt somehow helpless to check the advance of the stranger's progress without actual physical force. But she had reckoned without Ellen, who had been sizing up this apparently innocent intruder from her first entry into the room.

At the door of the living room, the way was blocked by Ellen's huge bulk, and with a suggestive finger she pointed toward the door.

"This house ain't open for inspection today, ma'am," she remarked, "and ye'd best be leavin' at wanst if yer foot is better. Mr. Trott will be home termorrer and ye can see him then if it's so important!" Ellen's words were like a physical push in the direction of the great outdoors. The woman glared at her, muttered a brief "Thank you" to Lois, opened the door, and hurried down the steps. In another moment she had climbed into her car, started it, and disappeared down the street. Lois stared after her in some wonderment.

"Why—she—she didn't *limp* at all!" she marveled to Ellen, who stood beside her watching the departure.

"Well—and why should she?" muttered that worthy. " 'Twas all a trick so she could get in here. The wurrld is full of them fakers! It's lucky I was here to steer her out the door!" And Ellen retired grumbling to her kitchen again.

Lois went back to her seat on the steps, but the spell of the earlier morning was broken, and her mind now dwelt only on the strange, unwelcome visitor and her wily ruse to enter the forbidden premises. It struck Lois that though the woman pretended to know little about the place, she seemed strangely familiar with the interior of the house, once she was inside. She evidently knew there were things on exhibition in the dining room across the hall. Perhaps she had seen them on some former visit, though it was only rarely that anyone was admitted to the house. But why should she think there were things on exhibition upstairs? It was all very puzzling and rather unpleasant. Lois gave it up finally and went to her room to practice the Chopin "Fantasie Impromptue."

Jean returned from school that afternoon bursting with news. She flung her books on the floor in their room and threw herself down by Lois, who was reading.

"Sandy's got a brother!" she panted. "He's a student at Rutgers College. He came home last night on his motor-bike. He's taking some sort of special course there, so he doesn't have to be on hand all the time. He's awfully nice and jolly. I saw him around outside just now. And Mrs. Coleman called me in and gave us all some doughnuts. She's nice, too. Why don't you get acquainted with her, Lois? Sandy says he can ride on Tim's motorcycle and he's going to teach me how."

"You'll do nothing of the sort!" exclaimed Lois, suddenly sitting up and taking notice. "Do you think we want you to have an accident and get all smashed up? Don't you *dare* ride that thing!"

"All right, all right!" giggled Jean. "Don't get all hot 'n' bothered about it. Sandy says Tim wouldn't allow it anyway. I only said it for fun—to get a rise out of you. You looked so sort of stupid, lying there mouching over that book. Mrs. Coleman says she's coming over to call tomorrow. She's meant to right along, only she's been so busy. She's nice—and so is Tim. You'll like 'em. No style—just nice comfy sort of folks."

Lois smiled inwardly at Jean's description of their neighbors and mentally decided that she'd reserve her own opinion till after the heralded call of state. But that afternoon, late, when Mr. Trott and Zeph had returned with a load of furniture, Tim Coleman strolled over to help unload it, as he often did when he was around. It interested him to talk to Silas Trott and see some of the queer articles that he often picked up. After the load was stored, Silas Trott brought the young fellow in and introduced him to Lois and Ellen.

Lois liked him from the first—liked his carroty red hair, his wide, friendly grin, his keen sense of humor. He promised to come over in the morning and bring a new book he thought she might like, and then took his departure, as it was getting near dinnertime.

When he was gone, Lois told Mr. Trott of the odd, unwelcome visitor they had had that morning, and remarked that if it hadn't been for Ellen she didn't know what the woman might have managed to walk away with. She had thought that Mr. Trott would make some smiling comment and then forget the subject, but to her great surprise he stood knitting his brows in thought, and finally asked gravely:

"Can thee describe her to me, Lois? I have a reason for asking."

Lois described the woman as best she could, wondering why he seemed so concerned. Then he warned her:

"It is as I feared. Thee must never admit this person to the house. I know her—and I have reason for making this request. Do not ask me to explain it, please. I can only tell thee this woman would cause us trouble—but not in any way thee may think. Should she come again when I am not here, keep Ellen by thee and send her away, no matter what her pretext." He did not elucidate the matter any further, but turned and went into his room. Lois thought he seemed very much disturbed.

"I wonder what it's all about?" she meditated. "More mystery! This house seems to have more than its share of them!"

6. Some Sidelights on Silas Trott

INDIAN summer still lingered in Herbertstown. Again it lay like a golden haze over the one quiet street of the little village, a morning or two later, and Lois, basking again on the tiny front porch, could not bear to go indoors and miss it. There was something so different from the accustomed chilly New England atmosphere at this season that it fascinated her just to be out of doors and reveling in it. She had not been there long when she was joined by Tim Coleman from across the street, who strolled over and plumped down on the steps at her feet.

"Sleepy old burg, isn't it!" he commented, whittling away at a stick. "Bet you never saw anything like it where *you* came from!"

"No, I didn't," admitted Lois. "I'd always thought our old New England town was small and sleepy enough, but it was wide-awake and stirring compared to this. But I *like* this, though. It's like the queer little old Southern towns that drowse all day in the sun and where nothing ever happens."

"Don't you fool yourself that nothing ever happens here!" contradicted Tim darkly. "Plenty has in the past, at times —and right in the house where you're living now!"

"It *has?*" cried Lois, thoroughly startled. "Oh, do tell me about it! I've had a feeling all along that there's something strange and secret about this place but have never had an explanation of it—and I somehow don't like to question Uncle Si."

"No, I wouldn't ask him if I were you," answered Tim gravely. "Somehow the queer things seem to be connected with him, and I think he's kind of sensitive about it all. And the present generation isn't supposed to know about it anyway. Only Mother's lived here a long time, and she's seen a lot. And once in a while she's told me a bit about things. She isn't a gossip, though, so she never retails it to outsiders."

"Well, do tell me about it," begged Lois. "That is, if you think she won't mind."

"Is Mr. Trott around?" asked Tim, glancing about him uneasily.

"No, he's gone to the garage somewhere or other, with Zeph, to have the truck fixed."

"Okay, then!" smiled Tim. "I'd hate to think he might be within hearing when I'm telling you this past history. I know he doesn't like to have it spoken of—at any rate when he's around. Well, to begin with, I wonder how much you know about your neighbors, outside of ourselves—the rest of the crowd that lives in this little town, I mean."

"Oh, nothing at all!" acknowledged Lois. "You see, we haven't been here very long, and we've been so busy getting settled—and I've been so sort of depressed—and nobody's called on us—and so we haven't really seen anyone except your mother. I've really not been away from this house, except to take a little walk occasionally, since we came. What kind of people are they, anyway?"

"You'd be surprised!" grinned Tim. "Outside of our

family, and Mr. Trott, and old Gedney Stevens, who keeps the general store and post office, there isn't a native-born American living in the place!" Lois looked considerably startled.

"There *isn't?*" she breathed incredulously. "But—but how can that be? Where have they all gone? Who lives here, anyhow?"

"I told you you'd be surprised!" chuckled Tim. "But it's an actual fact. These twenty or more houses really were built and lived in by genuine dyed-in-the-wool New Jersey people from 'way, 'way back. And they all lived here till a few years ago. But somehow this little old town never seemed to grow or get in any of the new improvements or keep up with the times. And so, one by one, the old families sort of drifted away from here and went to bigger towns. I suppose it was their young folks growing up and wanting to be in bigger schools and where more life was going on. Anyway, Herbertstown got left behind in the push. We would have gone ourselves a few years ago, but Father died and didn't leave much but the house and land, and I had to work through college, and Mother has just enough to keep us going, till I get out and start hustling. Then we'll probably move away, too. Old Ged Stevens, though, will no doubt hang on till the last trump! He'd just die if he didn't have his store and post office to take care of."

"But, tell me," interrupted Lois, "who *does* live in all the rest of these houses, anyway? I've scarcely ever seen anyone going in or out of them—perhaps I haven't noticed or cared much. But they all look inhabited—somebody must be in them."

"Oh, yes, they're inhabited, all right," Tim assured her. "But now it's almost entirely by foreigners—Polish and

Russian farmers and so on. They've come over here and bought the old farms from the American owners, and they spend most of their time in the fields behind these houses. Their wives help them, and the children—there aren't so many—go to school, and then work in the fields when they come home. Queer, isn't it?"

"That explains," mused Lois, "what Jean said, the first day she went to school in the bus. She said all the children except Sandy looked like foreigners. I thought it was rather strange."

"Yes, that's the situation, exactly," reiterated Tim. "It came about gradually—first one, then another of the old families sold their places and moved till now we're the only ones left. Mr. Trott had bought this place some years before the exodus began. It had belonged to a family named Slater, but they'd all died off, and the property was up for sale, and he bought it and moved in and began this queer old furniture-collecting."

"Then *he* didn't live here originally either," commented Lois. "It's odd, but I know so little about him. Supposed he'd always had this place. You see, he was a family friend, but I never heard Dad speak of him. Never knew of his existence, in fact, till he wrote to us after Dad's death and offered us a home. He must have kept track of us *somehow,* though. But what was the odd thing that happened here?—you were going to tell me about it."

"Do you see that little brick house over there in the fields?" Tim indicated a small, old-fashioned brick building of quaint architecture on his side of the street, far back from the road and reached only by a narrow lane running back to it some distance beyond the Coleman house. "Well, that house has had some queer connection with this place in the past—I mean Mr. Trott's house. Mother says some years ago—I don't even remember it myself, and I'm nearly twenty—that house was empty, had been for several years, and was finally hired by some city people named Brown, who said they planned to use it mainly as a sort of hunting lodge during the shooting season. It appeared to be a man and his wife and friends of theirs who came in and went at all sorts of odd hours, but, as far as Mother could see, never did any hunting at all. Curiously enough, Mr. Trott didn't seem to like 'em. They used to come over frequently and tried to look over his stock of junk and things, but he'd never let 'em in. Mother thought they seemed to be watching him, somehow.

"Then, all of a sudden, one night, there was an awful to-do right here in this house. Mother was the only outsider who happened to see it—and that was by accident! She'd waked up in the night and noticed lights on in this house. And as it was very late, and she knew Mr. Trott always went to bed rather early, she got up and looked out of the window. It was a queer sight she saw. Mr. Trott was standing on the doorstep—right here where we're sitting—and facing him were two people. Mother couldn't tell very well who they were because it was so dark. But she got to the window just in time to hear Mr. Trott address one of the group. And these, she declares, were his very words:

"'You know I am a Quaker—and unarmed. I do not believe in physical violence. But let this be understood between us—never will I agree to the proposal you make—and never will you succeed in this quest, whether I be dead or alive. You have weapons—use them now upon me if you choose. Or go about other business and leave me to mine!'

"And after that speech, Mother says he just stood there facing them and evidently dared them to shoot. She was scared simply speechless, but after a minute or two of whispering together, the bunch just faded away and left him standing. When they were out of sight down the road, where they'd evidently left a car, he turned and went indoors. The lights went out shortly afterward and the show was over. But Mother felt sure it was those same people who had rented that little brick house. They never came near the place again, and after a while she heard that Silas Trott had bought that brick house from the owners and had just shut it up and left it as it was, so that nobody that was objectionable to him could get possession of it again. Queer business, wasn't it? There was never any explanation of the little picnic on the front porch here that night, and Mother has been wondering about it ever since."

The recital left Lois marveling also, and she was suddenly impelled to tell Tim about the singular woman who had tried—and had succeeded—to get into the house a day or two before, while Mr. Trott was away. It was then Tim's turn to be surprised.

"It strikes me that it might be perhaps the same woman who was mixed up in the other affair," he hazarded. "Has he seemed worried about anything since?"

"You never can tell—with Uncle Si," said Lois. "He always seems so calm and unruffled and undisturbed, no matter what happens. But I notice that he hasn't gone away from the town for any length of time since. That may not mean a thing, though, except that he hasn't discovered any more old furniture to buy."

"Odd business, too—this old-furniture racket of his!" observed Tim. "He doesn't carry it out on the usual lines at all. Three quarters of the stuff he has around here is just plain rubbish—the worst kind of old junk. According to the code of regular antique dealers, he'd be considered the most

awful flop. I've seen him sell for ten cents a thing you'd pay
two or three dollars for in a regular antique place, and on
the other hand charge a woman a quarter for a secondhand
baking tin. She could have bought a much better one brand-
new in any five-and-ten. There doesn't seem to be any
rhyme or reason to it! But I've pretty well made up my
mind that old Silas has some other game up his sleeve that
is only remotely connected with all this."

Suddenly Lois sat bolt upright and faced Tim, still whittling on his stick of wood, which now presented a very
clever replica of the hull of a catboat, and exclaimed:

"Oh, I've just had a wonderful idea! Something you
were saying a moment ago made me think—"

But at that instant a truck rumbled down the peaceful
sunlit street, and Tim put a restraining hand on her arm.

"Here come Mr. Trott and Zeph," he warned. "Better
save what you were going to say till another time. There's
still quite a bit I haven't told you about all this!" And Lois
accepted his hint and began talking of something else.

7. The Little Red Brick House

A DULL, cloudy Saturday afternoon—and nothing to do!
Such was the verdict of Jean, curled up disconsolately on
the couch in the bedroom, trying to interest herself in an
ancient and very tattered copy of *David Copperfield* that
she had found in one of the furniture sheds on the floor,
amid hundreds of other ancient and even more dilapidated

volumes. She could hear Ellen banging about cheerfully in the kitchen, crooning her own peculiar version of "Killarney." A delicious smell of baking gingerbread was wafted up through the hall. Lois was out with Tim in the Coleman Ford coupé, having been invited to go on a trip to Trenton. Jean had not been asked, much to her outspoken disgust. Uncle Si and Zeph were away for the day with the furniture truck. She was even bereft of the company of Sandy, whose determined mother had insisted that his Monday homework must be done at this and no other time, she knowing full well that otherwise it wouldn't be done at all!

It had been such an interesting morning! The sun had been bright, and she and Sandy had invented a marvelous new game, out in the cluttered yard of the house. This had been inspired by one of Uncle Si's descriptions of an auction he had recently attended, where the bidding for certain choice pieces of furniture had been close, high, and very exciting. He had promised to take them all to an auction sometime and let them gather the interest of it for themselves. Meantime she and Sandy had invented one of their own. With incredible exertion, they had gathered and dragged to one spot a quantity of the decrepit and useless odds and ends that were lying about. Then, from the platform in front of the largest storage shed, which they had used as an auctioneer's block, they had carried on an extemporaneous auction of their own, taking turns at being auctioneer and purchaser, and pretending much competitive bidding from imaginary rivals. Uncle Si had come out to watch them and had laughingly taken part in the game, showing some of the tricks used on both sides. Even Zeph had joined in the fun, and Ellen and Lois had watched from the kitchen door. Yes, it had been a marvelous morning—only to descend into the anticlimax of this dreary and lonely afternoon!

Jean began to stare out of the window, the book lying forgotten in her lap. There was nothing much in sight but the Coleman house directly across the street. Even Sandy was not visible. She knew he must be hunched over his books by the kitchen table, his mother helping him while she did her Saturday baking. Off to the left, across the meadow beside the Coleman house, well back from the road and half hidden by low-drooping weeping-willow trees, she could glimpse the odd little red brick house with the white door, and heavy white shutters that were always tightly closed and barred. There was something about this tightly shuttered house that had intrigued her from the very first. She had questioned Sandy about it, but he had not seemed very well informed on the subject. Nobody lived in it— that much he knew. But as to whom it belonged, how long it had been shut and barred, whether anyone ever came to open it or go in or out, he apparently knew nothing. She had found Mrs. Coleman better informed, when she had questioned her on the subject one day. Mrs. Coleman had declared that, as far as she knew, Mr. Silas Trott owned the house, but she thought it was empty. And that was all the information Jean could extract.

But still the little red brick house intrigued her—shut up, barred, silent. Why was it so? And if Uncle Si owned it, why didn't he open it and use it for *some* purpose or other? What was the *good* of a house barred and shuttered in that useless fashion? Maybe there was something queer about it—maybe it was *haunted!* A delicious, shivery suspicion! Suddenly Jean threw her book aside and sat up straight. She had it—a tremendously exciting way to spend the rest of the afternoon. She would slip out, all by herself, and explore that house—if there were any possible way she could wriggle into it. After all, if it was Uncle Si's house, the same as her home, there could be no possible objection. It was not like breaking into some stranger's property!

With Jean, to plan was to act—with as much celerity as possible. She got on her beret and sweater and tiptoed downstairs, devoutly hoping Ellen would not hear her and question her exit, or drag her in to help beat up cake dough or mix the icing. That would spoil everything. When would she ever have as free an opportunity for the adventure as *this* afternoon afforded?

But the stairs creaked betrayingly, and Ellen's voice came booming through the hall: "Where you goin', Tiny?" (Jean had always been "Tiny" to Ellen, ever since she was born.)

"Oh, just out a little while!" caroled Jean bravely making a bolt for the front door. (She usually sallied forth through the kitchen, grabbing any loose eatable that was lying about, on the way!)

"Look here!—it's goin' to rain—any minute!" roared Ellen warningly. "I won't have you gettin' wet and catchin'——"

But Jean stayed to hear no more. And the front door slammed on Ellen's warning. "If it rains, I'll come in —or maybe I'll be able to get in the little house—so it's all right, anyway!" she consoled herself and salved her conscience for slipping out on Ellen. And lest she be waylaid and hauled in by an irate Ellen emerging through the kitchen door, she darted swiftly across the street, slipped around behind the Coleman house on the side least used by the family, and was speedily out of sight behind the thick bushes that lined the lane to the little red house.

One thing she had known before but had never happened to investigate very thoroughly—the little red house faced on a fair-sized stream that meandered through the woods and meadows over a clear red-clay and pebble-bottomed bed. Just in front of the house it was wider than elsewhere, and there was a narrow, pebbly beach over which the willows hung protectingly. Across the stream thick woods grew down to the very edge, and tiny fish darted about in the clear shallows. A lovely place to wade and possibly corral some of those tiny fish for her aquarium, meditated Jean. But not today. It was too dark and lowering, and the threatened rain had already begun. Besides, there were other more important matters on hand.

She turned and circled the little house slowly, keeping a weather eye out for any possible crevice or opening that promised an entrance to the intriguing spot. But apparently there was none. All shutters within reach were tightly barred and fastened, evidently on the inside. There was a little white porch running across the side facing the stream, and a heavy white front door opened on it. This too was uncompromisingly locked. Even a sloping cellar door at the back had a padlock strong enough for a bank vault ornamenting it, and there were no cellar windows in the foundation.

It had now begun to rain in real earnest, and Jean was on the point of giving up, in furious and tearful despair, when something she had hitherto overlooked caught her eye. On the little front porch, a latticework vine trellis ran from the railing to the roof of the porch. The vine it had once supported had long since vanished, but the trellis provided toeholds that would make its ascent, to a person no heavier than Jean, not entirely impossible. With the big drops of rain pelting down on her, she grasped the support and waveringly began the ascent.

Halfway up, she did not think she would ever be able to make it. She was sure she must either let go her hold and jump for safety or go crashing to the ground with the wreck of the thing when it gave way, as it threatened to, and collapsed. But two more toeholds at last gave her a grasp on the roof of the porch, and she clawed her way upward to safety, monkey-like, finally getting one knee over the edge of the porch roof.

"When I go down," she promised herself, "I'll shinny down one of the posts. I won't trust to that trellis again!" And she found herself perched on the gently sloping roof, within easy reach of the nearest closed shutters of the upper floor.

"Suppose it'll be just my luck to find these as tight as the others—and after all that climb, too!" she muttered, poking gingerly at the shutter of the nearest window. Her prediction was so far correct. The shutter was as immovable as any of the others had been. She edged cautiously along the sloping shingles of the roof, her rubber-soled sneakers keeping her from slipping, and reached the farther window. Inserting her hand under the edge of the shutter, she shook it, without any hope that it would be different from the rest.

Then she had the surprise of her life! The shutter seemed looser than the other, and though it only bowed when she jerked at it, the glaring fact became apparent—that it was *not* fastened on the inside! With a low whoop of delight, Jean tore at it, and presently its edge parted from that of its mate with a protesting jerk and swung open, revealing an unshaded, uncurtained window behind it. And before she looked within, Jean was interested enough to note that the iron hook which had caught the shutter on the inside had completely rusted through—doubtless from some rain

drip of the eaves above—and that was the explanation of
the ease with which it had come open. Then she pressed her
nose against the windowpane and tried to stare into the
room.

In the dim gloom of the waning, rainy afternoon, and
with the reflection of outdoors on the glass, she was able
to perceive little or nothing of the interior. But she had
come provided for just such an emergency as this.

From the pocket of her sweater she extracted a tiny
flashlight and turned it in toward the darkening interior and once again flattened her nose against the pane.
For several long moments she kept it there, turning the light
about to illuminate every black corner. And when she had
seen it all, she leaned back on her heels and indulged in a
low whistle of complete amazement.

"Well!—if this isn't the *queerest!*" she muttered. "I'm
glad I came—and I'm glad I came alone. This is going to
be *my* secret—from now on. I don't believe I'll even tell
Sandy!"

With utmost caution she closed the shutters again, put
her flashlight back in her pocket, lowered herself cautiously
to a corner of the roof, and, wrapping her knees about the
porch pillar, shinnied skillfully down to safety. Then, lowering her head and ducking through the steady downpour,
she made a beeline back to the house, prepared to face an
irate Ellen, but with the firm determination in her heart to
tell no one what she had seen through the window of the
little red house!

8. Ellen Has Her Suspicions

THE MILD, Indian summer days were over, and the cold, dreary rains of late November had set in. Thanksgiving had come and gone, and Ellen, true to her New England training, had insisted on a turkey and the "fixings," which Silas Trott had approved with enthusiasm and pronounced the best and only turkey he had eaten in years. Even Zeph had condescended to a wide and brilliant grin as he gnawed his drumstick with deep content in the kitchen. Later he had confided to Ellen, "Yo're the best cook I seen since I left Alabam' when I wuz a kid." And she had replied tersely, "Go 'long with that blarney! Do ye want some more giblet gravy?" But the affair had cemented an unspoken truce between them.

Gradually, insidiously and quite unnoticed, Ellen had managed to effect a thorough cleaning of the kitchen, living room (in which the family ate at a long refectory table), and had now made her way into the dining room, so long unused for eating purposes, but devoted to being the cluttered showroom for glass, china, metal articles, and like accumulated secondhands, by Silas Trott. The room had always irked her, with its dirt and dust of years, the cluttered and broken or otherwise absolutely useless trash that lay about mixed in with intact and really worth-while stuff. She had figured it out that if she could manage to clean even so much as a little corner of it in off moments when Silas was not about, she might in time, without his noticing it, get the whole into a more sanitary and tidy condition. It seemed a hopeless task, and if Silas found her at it he would doubtless put an instant end to her cleansing ministrations. But gradually the room was beginning to emerge into a more ordered state. If Silas noticed the gradual metamorphosis, he gave no sign, and Ellen waxed bolder in her cleaning excursions with every unmolested day.

She was at it one dark and rainy morning when Lois was upstairs practicing, Jean safely at school, and Silas out with Zeph on some mysterious errand with the furniture truck. Having finished the corner she had allotted as the morning's work, ranged the bright and freshly polished glassware on a clean end of the long table, and swept and refurbished the floor in the vicinity, she suddenly bethought herself that the time was ripe for a beginning on Silas Trott's own bedroom which was on that same floor. His rugs were heavy with dust and trodden-in gravel. His windows needed cleaning, and the wooden floor should have the first scrubbing it had known in years. But all this could not be done at once—that would be too noticeable. She would do the floor and shake the rugs today. The rest could come later. Silas allowed her to make his bed and tidy up a bit, every day, but more he had never consented to, saying that he preferred it as it was.

Ellen went to the kitchen, got a fresh pail of warm water and a broom, then marched across the hall and boldly opened the door of Silas Trott's own private domain. She had made the bed earlier in the morning before he went away, so she was free to turn her attention at once to the task in hand. She decided at first to gather up the dusty rugs, take them to the side porch, which was roofed and sheltered from the rain, and beat and sweep them there. And this she proceeded to do. But one, in front of the bureau, was caught under the foot of that piece of furniture, and it required some lifting and struggling to get it free. As she bent over to accomplish this, her eye was caught by a piece of paper lying in full view on the bureau, scrawled over in the large and somewhat sprawling handwriting that Silas usually affected when writing without his glasses. And though Ellen was the soul of honor about reading any personal writing that did not concern her, she could not help but take in the words as she bent over to lift the leg of the bureau. The words she saw were these:

"*Another clue gone wrong.*
Try Ballantyne 4408."

That was all, but it made Ellen's eyes pop open wide, and she muttered, as she stood staring at it: "Now what—in the name of all the saints—does *that* mean?"

It was a very hopeless question. It might mean anything—sinister or perfectly innocuous, for all Ellen knew. Under ordinary circumstances she would have passed it by as some very harmless note made by Silas Trott to remind him of something that might easily slip his memory. But circumstances in this house were not "ordinary." Ellen had eyes in her head, and she had been using them of late for more than just her usual puttering about the kitchen or cleaning up elsewhere. There were curious things going on —things you couldn't explain by passing them off as the ordinary events of even so unconventional a household as Silas Trott's. She had early sensed that there was more to this secondhand furniture business than met the eye. And what was the meaning of that locked room on the upper floor, and Mr. Silas Trott's nocturnal comings and goings into and out of it when the household was supposed to be sound asleep? Oh, she had heard them—but she had not referred to them, especially to her blessed "children," for she did not wish to alarm them unnecessarily. But you couldn't fool Ellen McConkey long! She knew, when she was living in a household run on such peculiar lines, that all was not normal.

Then there was the matter of those curious things Zeph had said at various odd times when she had fed him more than usually well and he was in an expansive mood.

"What makes Mr. Trott keep such a funny house, like?" she had inquired casually of Zeph a morning or two previously, while he was gorging luxuriously, on a huge plate of Ellen's famous griddle cakes and maple syrup. Zeph, she had found, could always be made to talk when he was being more than usually well fed!

"Yo' kin search me!" he had replied, swallowing an enormous mouthful of griddle cake. "It's bin like that ever since I come with him years an' years ago. Always this mess roun' an' him always hangin' roun' auctions, buying a lot er truck he don't want nor need nor ain't goin' ter sell." Zeph helped himself to another steaming cake from a fresh pile just off the griddle.

"Tell yo' what, though," he added, plying them with butter and maple syrup. "I seen a lot that the ol' man ain't no idee I kotched on to, an' I got my 'pinion whut's goin' on— that man's *lookin' fo' somethin'!* Lookin' all the time— huntin' in them auctions, buying things he don't want, ransackin' 'em—I seen him at it mo'n once!" Ellen felt now that Zeph was sufficiently started, and she suddenly switched to another puzzling theme.

"What do ye make out he keeps that room upstairs all locked fer?" she questioned casually. "That room makes me plum mad—it does! I hate ter think of a room needin' a cleanin' as long as that must of, an' me never havin' a chance to get in an' do it."

"Don't fool yo'self," Zeph warned her mysteriously. "Yo' ain't goin' ter git inter that room, woman, so long as Mr. Silas Trott's alive."

"An' why *not*?" she demanded, pretending indignation. "It must be filthy by this time."

"Make no difference whut it look like—yo' ain't never goin' be 'lowed in it!" prophesied Zeph. "Me, I ain't never had my nose so much as near the crack. But lemme tell you one t'ing." He lowered his voice to a tone of hushed mystery. "I know whut there *ain't* in that room—*not one hones'-truth speck of furniture*—there ain't! An' yo' kin make what you like of that!" Ellen stared at him almost bereft of speech.

"For the love of heaven!" she breathed at length. "What do you think of *that!* But how did ye know it, Zeph?"

" 'Cause once when Mr. Silas wuz away for the day an' I stayed home, a right bad thunderstorm come up an' a high wind. An' that wind jes' tore one o' them shutters loose, an' it wuz bangin' away like it wuz gonna come off. I hadda git right up an' fix it before it tore loose an' fell. An' when I was up there an' the shutter loose, of course I done looked in the winder—ain't no law agin that—an' there I done saw it—not one stick—not even a chair—the room jes' plumb *empty!*"

"Then what's he runnin' in an' out of it all the time for?" marveled Ellen. "There don't seem no sense to it."

"There *ain't* no sense—but it ain't none o' your business —or mine neither," counseled Zeph philosophically.

Ellen had had to agree that it wasn't, but just the same the question had teased her with its unanswered riddle ever since. And here before her now was another side to the enigma. Silas himself makes a note about some mysterious "clue" and thoughtlessly leaves it out on his bureau in full sight. Ellen whiled away her evenings with occasional detective magazines, so she was not unacquainted with "clues" and their mysterious import. She stood now, leaning on the bureau, cudgeling her brains for an answer—but none came. Whatever "clue" Silas Trott was on the track of was, and probably would remain, hidden from her. But why had he left this note right out in plain sight, if he was so anxious that his affairs should remain hidden? Suddenly two reasons occurred to her—one of them rather disturbing.

Silas Trott had either intended to take the slip of paper with him, or else he had left it where it was, knowing that, since Ellen had made his bed and tidied up earlier in the day, no one was supposed to enter his room until the following morning. Hence, anything he left about should be safe from prying eyes. Ellen's conscience suddenly smote her.

"It's not right I am—poking about his room when he doesn't know it—even if it is so dusty an' me only wantin' to clean it up! An', what's more, if he comes in an' finds it clean, he'll know right well that I've been in here an' probably seen that private note he left lyin' about. Ellen McConkey, ye'd best get right out of this here, if ye know what's healthy fer ye!"

And grabbing up her pail and broom, she fled to the safe and unforbidden precincts of the kitchen.

9. A Sound in the Night

IT HAPPENED so suddenly that none of them quite realized its import at first—the thing that was to make such a change in the whole routine of their lives. Christmas had come and gone. It had not been a very enlivening period for the girls, filled, as it could not help but be, with saddened memories of the year before when their father had been with them and life was still pursuing its normal course. Ellen, too, was depressed but strove to hide as much as possible of it from her charges. Silas Trott and Zeph, not having made any special event of that holiday for many a long year, were more unconcerned about it, though Silas ordered Ellen to prepare another turkey and presented the girls with a couple of gifts he had selected from his stock of "antiques"; to Lois a quaint and quite beautiful mahogany corner cupboard in which to stack her books, and to Jean a pretty little Governor Winthrop desk where she might dispose of her school things and study and write. For Ellen he had found a delightfully comfortable and deeply cushioned lounging chair for her room, with a small side table to go with it.

His thought for them touched them all, for they realized that he was not accustomed to Christmas giving, having had apparently no one in many long years upon whom to bestow such gifts. They felt that their own little Christmas remembrances to him were quite inadequate, but none of them had any special money to spend. Yet in his quiet way he expressed himself as being inordinately pleased with his knit worsted bed slippers from Ellen, his half-dozen finely hemstitched linen handkerchiefs that Lois had spent her hours over, and the hand-painted collar box that Jean had devised, partly out of her own head and partly from instructions learned at school.

But the real Christmas celebration had been enjoyed over at the home of the Colemans, where the holiday spirit waxed high. Mrs. Coleman believed in the tree, the stocking-hanging, the decoration with greens and holly, and all the old-time customs being rigidly observed. And with Tim home for the holidays and Sandy rampantly loose from school, and the insistence of Mrs. Coleman that her neighbors across the street share in many of the festivities, this side of a Herbertstown Christmas had gone far toward lifting the spirits of the three newcomers to the neighborhood. On Christmas night she had given a party to which her neighbors across the street had all been invited. Even Zeph grinned at the goings-on from the doorway and helped to serve the chicken salad, ice cream, and cake later. Tim had found and presented his mother with a rather old-fashioned but still in-good-working-order battery radio (there being no electricity in town, so that the newer type was impossible to use), and they had Christmas music and the young folks danced, while their elders smilingly looked on. Old Gedney Stevens, postmaster and general storekeeper, was the only other outside guest, and he astonished everyone at the end of the evening by getting up and dancing "Turkey in the Straw" and then dropping back in his chair fiery red from exertion and embarrassment at his own daring. Lois confided to Tim that she hadn't half appreciated old Gedney Stevens up to the present.

"Oh, he's a grand old bird, is Gedney!" chuckled Tim. "You don't half know his good points yet." She didn't, but in the very near future she was to learn the genuine worth of old Gedney.

The dawn of the day after Christmas was heralded by a severe, three-day northeaster of cold, sleety rain, icy winds, and general discomfort. Yet in spite of it Silas went off with Zeph that morning to a special auction sale over at Moorestown, from which even the inclement weather could not keep him away. He returned toward evening, soaked and shivering, but insisted on remaining outdoors to help Zeph put away the newly purchased furniture in the biggest shed.

Ellen prophesied that he would have a cold, but he laughed at her fears even while he drank a bowl of hot beef tea and then went to change his drenched clothing before the evening meal. He seemed very pleased with something that had happened that day, though he did not enlighten them as to what it might be. Then he had gone to his room and remained there the rest of the evening.

Somehow, that night, Lois could not get to sleep. The rain slatted against the windows of her room with a vicious strength, and the wind tore through the tree branches in a wild, wailing accompaniment. An unreasoning foreboding chilled her and drove sleep from her, while the grandfather's clock in the hall downstairs chimed one hour after another. Long after midnight, she heard the stealthy sound of tiptoeing feet ascending the stairs and slipping down the hall. And she knew it to be Silas Trott, on one of his occasional nightly pilgrimages to the mysterious room at the end of the hall. What could he be doing in that strange room at this weird hour? she marveled. And she lay awake till she heard the clock chime two. Then she must have dozed a bit.

Suddenly she woke from a light nap with a jerk and sat straight up in bed. What was it that had roused her?

All was silence and darkness in the house, though the wind and rain still raged outside. Perhaps it was only some loose shutter that had banged and wakened her. She was about to settle down again, when there came a strange sound from the direction of the hall. It was something between a groan and a faint call, and this time she jumped straight out of bed, threw on her silk-wadded wrapper, and thrust her feet into feather-pomponned mules. Then with shaking fingers she groped for her flashlight which she always kept under her pillow, tiptoed across the floor, and softly opened the door into the hall.

The sight that flashed to her in the beam of her flashlight was alarming. For on the floor, directly outside the partly closed door of the mysterious room, lay Silas Trott, breathing harshly and rapidly, clutching his chest with both hands, and unquestionably suffering horribly. She ran and knelt beside him and laid a cold hand on his forehead—to find it burning hot beyond belief.

"Oh, Uncle Si," she breathed, "*what* is the matter? What can I do for you?" He seemed to rouse himself with a mighty effort.

"Get Ellen—get Zeph!" he croaked hoarsely and relapsed into ghastly shivering and semiconsciousness again.

Lois flew into Ellen's room, shaking her awake and explaining breathlessly what had happened. And while Ellen was struggling into some clothes, she darted back to her own room, dragged a raincoat and galoshes from her closet, got into them, rushed downstairs and out to Zeph's shed, where she hammered on the door and shouted to him to dress and come in at once. She did one thing more before returning to the house. Struggling through the drenching downpour and wind, she groped her way across the street, jangled the bell of the Coleman house again and again till she had roused the sleeping members, shouted up to Tim, who poked his inquiring head from his window, a brief word of the emergency, and at last fled back to the shelter of her own abode.

The rest of the hours till morning seemed a wild nightmare that she could only be struggling through in a dream. Ellen and Zeph and Tim gathered almost simultaneously, and together they all managed to get the heavy body of Silas downstairs and into his own bedroom and at last into his bed. Then Tim had hurried away to get his mother's car and drive to the nearest town where a good doctor could be found, there being none in Herbertstown. And in the interval before his return, they did what they could, commanded by Ellen, who had had a full experience with illness, to ease the suffering of the stricken man. Mrs. Coleman also had joined them and lent her own suggestions to the cause.

"It's jest as I knew!" muttered Ellen, preparing a mustard plaster in the kitchen. "'Tis a chill he has—an' the saints only know what beside—an' lucky he'll be if he ain't got the new-mon-i-aye! Didn't I *tell* him he was temptin' Providence this very night—an' him laughin' at me!" And so on and so on, while Lois tiptoed in and out distractedly, got in the way, and was bidden to go back to bed and try to sleep.

But bed and sleep were not for Lois, and she roamed through the house and peered out of the windows, praying that Tim would be successful in speedily capturing a doctor. Only Jean, whom none of them had thought it wise to waken, slept peacefully through the turmoil of the night. Then there was a sound in the street outside, and Lois rushed to the door to admit Tim—and a doctor carrying the usual satchel, looking sleepy and quite impersonally pro-

fessional, as he inquired which room the patient was oc-
cupying. Then he disappeared into the room and the door
was shut tight for a long, long while.

Lois and Tim, being shut out from the inner circle surrounding Silas, sat shivering in the living room, silent for
long spells or speculating in hushed whispers as to what
could be the trouble. Presently Tim went out to the wood-
pile, brought in an armful of logs, and finally succeeded in
coaxing into life a rousing fire on the open hearth, over
which they both crouched, drawing comfort and courage
from the cheering blaze.

"Tell me how all this happened," said Tim at length.
"Perhaps you don't realize it, but actually I haven't heard
a thing yet about how he came to be taken ill, or how
you first knew about it." And Lois had recounted to him
the startling way in which she had made her discovery. She
had just finished when Ellen poked her head out of Silas'
bedroom door and called to her.

"Mr. Trott, he jest come to for a minute—he's sort of out
of his head with pain most of the time—an' he seemed to be
worryin' about his bunch of keys. Says he thinks he left
'em in the door of the room upstairs an' wants 'em brought
down. You run an' get 'em like a good child, Lois. We've
got our hands full in here."

Obediently Lois started up the stairs and Tim came rac-
ing after her with her flashlight, which she had left on a
chair in the living room. Going down the hall together toward that end room, she whispered:

"That's the room I told you about—he keeps it always
locked up. So mysterious! I wonder—" Suddenly she stopped
short.

"Oh! *Look!* The door's wide open—it was never that
way before!"

"Probably he hadn't had time to lock it when he was taken with that awful pain," suggested Tim, "and then in some draft it uncaught and swung open. See—his keys are hanging from the lock!"

They approached the door, and Tim could not refrain, as he reached to close and lock it, from turning the flashlight into the forbidden room. And Lois, behind him, peered over his shoulder into the mysterious fastness that seemed to occupy so much of Silas Trott's secret attention. Then they both drew back and stared incredulously into each other's eyes.

"Good night!" breathed Tim. "*What* do you make of that room?"

The room was utterly and absolutely *empty,* except for one large and handsome oriental rug, covering most of the floor. The walls were covered with paneling in white woodwork, and there was a fireplace surrounded by a carved whitewood mantel. But even the fireplace was bare of grate or andirons, and the windows were blank with tightly barred solid wooden shutters. The whole effect was uncanny in the extreme.

"What does he *do* in here?" whispered Lois.

"That's just it!" echoed Tim. "It isn't so much that it's an empty room. There's nothing mysterious about such a thing in itself. But why keep it locked, refuse to talk about it, and come here only in the dead of night? Why, look! —there isn't even a closet door or a small cupboard—or a single place where anything could be hidden!" They stood marveling for an interval over the strange enigma of the empty room. Then Tim remembered the affairs of the moment.

"Well, we must lock it up and take down the keys. I suppose old Silas wouldn't have liked our peeking in here

—and we wouldn't have done it if the door had been shut —but you just couldn't *help* it under the circumstances." He drew the door shut, turned the key, and extracted the bunch. Then they both went back to the living room, and Lois handed the keys to Ellen, who had opened the bedroom door as she approached it.

"Thanks, darlin'. The poor old man's off again an' don't know a thing. The doctor jest give him a sleepin' powder. He's goin' to stay till mornin', an' then he says we'll have ter git a trained nurse. He'll try ter find one for us. I'll put these keys under Mr. Trott's pillow, so's he can find 'em when he gits awake. Now there ain't a single thing more you kin do, nor Tim neither. Mrs. Coleman an' Zeph an' me c'n take care of it all, an' the doctor's goin' to git some sleep on the couch in the livin' room, so's he c'n be handy in case of need. You jest send Tim home to bed an' go up to yer own. Ye c'n help out best by gittin' breakfast in the mornin' in case I'm busy." And Ellen, heavy-eyed with loss of sleep and anxiety, shut the door.

Tim lingered for a while, but when the weary doctor came in to snatch a nap on the couch, he too vanished, and Lois was left to trail disconsolately up to her own room where, worn out with anxiety and loss of sleep, she presently sank into uneasy slumber.

10. Starched Tyranny and Suspense

A WEEK of most acute anxiety, discomfort, and suspense followed. The doctor returned the next afternoon, bringing with him a trained nurse and, after much impressive ceremony, installed her in charge of the case. Miss Jenks was large, imposing, undoubtedly efficient, and starched to such a degree of stiffness that she fairly crackled when she moved about. She immediately ousted Ellen and Mrs. Coleman from the sickroom, and from that moment they did little else save take her orders and run about on endless errands. Mrs. Coleman finally retired to her own home and the needs of her family and Lois filled the vacancy and took orders with the indignant Ellen.

At first Ellen had been meek and obliging, humbly anxious to do whatever would be best for Mr. Trott's safety and comfort. The doctor had suggested that she relieve Miss Jenks for a few hours every afternoon, so that the nurse might have some extra sleep or go out for a walk. Otherwise she was free to go about her own affairs and duties. But Miss Jenks kept her running about so constantly that Lois at length volunteered to do the errands and let the conscientious Ellen get some rest. Secretly Lois knew that Ellen would not long endure this tyranny, and she dreaded the time when the McConkey temper should get the best of her, and the fur begin to fly.

There was no denying that Silas Trott was gravely ill. Even before the day of his exposure to the storm, he had been far from well, though with his usual reticence he had admitted it to no one. The drenching and long exposure had finished the work, and he lay now, delirious and unconscious, with the severest type of pneumonia, so the doctor said. And what the outcome would be, he refused to predict.

It was a saddened and despairing houshould that tried to go about its tasks in as normal a fashion as possible, though there was nothing normal or running in the accustomed fashion. Jean, free from school for the holidays, huddled, subdued and miserable, in her own room or got underfoot in the kitchen. Ellen finally sent her over to the Coleman's to amuse herself with Sandy and get her out of the way. Lois was too busy at unaccustomed tasks of dusting, dishwashing, and errand-running to have a moment to spare, even for her own thoughts, and she was rather glad of it. Anything was better than sitting about idle, a prey to nameless fears and apprehensions.

By the end of the first day it was perfectly obvious to everyone that Miss Jenks disapproved thoroughly of the whole establishment. She made it plain that lack of electricity and other conveniences was something she had never had to cope with before. Nor had she ever seen a house so full of conglomerate and ill-assorted furniture. And her condemning glances, as she went in and out and back and forth on her errands, were enough to sear the very walls and shrivel up the other inmates! Ellen complained of her secretly to the doctor, on his third visit, and wanted to know what she was so "snooty" about anyhow, and why didn't she tend to her own business and let other people's affairs alone?

"I know, I know!" sighed the doctor, resignedly. "She's that way, Ellen, and you'll just have to put up with it, because she's the best pneumonia nurse I've ever had and knows her business to a 'T.' So try to be as patient as you can, because she may be able to help me save the situation for Mr. Trott." And Ellen had humbly acquiesced!

Another situation that had to be met was the matter of the various people who strayed in occasionally to buy either the odds and ends of ordinary secondhand furniture or the genuine antiques. This was something that only Silas Trott himself had ever superintended. Tim Coleman volunteered to attend to this emergency. And, as he could not actually sell things without knowing their prices, he decided to send everyone away, saying Mr. Trott could not have any sales made till he himself could take charge again. So he took up his post in the living room and made himself useful in his own way.

To Tim in the living room, on the second afternoon, came Lois, who had just descended from the upper floor, where she had been trying to put her own and Jean's room in order after two days of disorder.

"Gosh, I'm glad to see someone!" he vouchsafed, a pleased smile rippling over his solemn countenance. "It's darned lonesome sitting here doing nothing, and all the rest of you so busy. I feel as if I ought to be helping in some other way, but there doesn't seem anything else I can do. No buyers have been around all day. It's still storming too hard, I reckon. How's Uncle Si?" Tim also called Mr. Trott "Uncle Si," having done so ever since he was a small boy.

"Just about the same—so they say," sighed Lois. "He doesn't seem to know anything most of the time. He's terribly ill!" She burst into sudden and quite unexpected tears, and Tim tried awkwardly to comfort her.

"Don't feel so bad!" he muttered. "They are always like

that—at first—with pneumonia—at least, so I've understood." Lois presently got herself in hand.

"Forgive me! I'm just awfully upset," she murmured, wiping her eyes. "I really didn't know till—till this happened—how fond I'd grown of Uncle Si. But, Tim, there's something that's bothering me, and I want to talk to you about it. The nurse, Miss Jenks, came out in the hall this morning and handed me this scrap of paper. She said she'd found it under Uncle Si's pillow, along with a bunch of keys. She'd put the keys in his bureau drawer but thought perhaps I ought to take charge of this. Didn't know whether it was important or not. I didn't think much of this at the time, but I remembered how fussy he'd been about his keys that first night and thought perhaps I'd better take charge of them too. So I asked her for them and she got them for me. I have them locked in my bureau now, so they will be safe.

"Then, later, I glanced over this paper" (she drew it from her pocket as she spoke), "and it seems to me very mysterious—and yet as if something ought to be done about it. You see it's been torn, so the whole of the writing isn't there. What do you make of it—and what ought we to do about it?" She put the paper in question into Tim's hand. He studied it curiously.

"H'm!—the back of an old envelope, evidently—torn off along one side—after it had been written on. I wonder how?"

"But see what it *says!*" pointed out Lois.

And this is what Tim saw: *"In case of my . . . sult G . . . locked ro . . ."* That was all—just a fragment in terribly scrawled and all but indecipherable writing, and only a part of some message or reminder, whatever the whole may have been.

"What do you think it means?" demanded Lois. "Oh, I *wish* it hadn't been torn, and we had the whole thing! Perhaps it's some message he wanted us to have."

"It looks as if it were," agreed Tim. "One thing is certain: he's referring in it to the 'locked room,' though all the last word isn't there. But it couldn't be anything else. And we know what room *that* is!"

"But what about the beginning?—'In case of my . . .'" inquired Lois.

"Looks to me as if it could mean only two things," said Tim gravely. "Either something about illness or being laid up sick—or that sort of thing—or else—his death. And I'm awfully afraid he meant—the latter."

"Oh, *why?*" questioned Lois, almost under her breath.

"Because of what comes next," he answered gently. "This part of a word—'sult'—comes at the beginning of the line, and seems to me can only be the part of one of two words— 'result' or 'consult.' The first one wouldn't mean 'Consult somebody or other whose name begins with 'G'. It looks very much to me as if he'd tried to write: 'In case of my death' (probably) 'consult G' (possibly) 'about the locked room.' Does that strike you as sensible?"

Lois had to admit that it did, and then demanded if anything should be done about it.

"Not a thing, at present," decided Tim. "To begin with, this is all guesswork on our part. And even if we had it right, Uncle Si may get over this all right and there'll be no occasion to use it. And we haven't the least idea who 'G' is anyway. Best thing to do is put it away safely with the keys and say nothing about it till there's some reason to."

"Thanks, Tim. I will," said Lois simply and left the room to carry out his suggestion.

The crisis came in the afternoon of the last day of the

year. All of the night before and the morning Silas Trott had lain in a heavy stupor, his rasping breathing audible in every part of the house. The doctor had been in attendance almost constantly, Miss Jenks went about her duties with a grave and preoccupied air, omitting even to complain about the inconveniences she was contending with, and the rest of the household crept about their affairs wet-eyed, speechless, almost holding their breath in the intensity of their anxiety and fear. Tim still held the fort in the living room. And since the weather had cleared a day or two before, he had had a number of times to turn away would-be purchasers.

Lois and Jean huddled there with him, finding comfort in his presence and holding themselves ready to execute the various errands demanded of them by Ellen or Miss Jenks. The early darkness drew down shortly after four, and Tim piled fresh logs on the open fire, while Lois lighted the old brass student lamp. They all crouched, voiceless, around the fire, straining their ears to catch every sound, though nothing came to them save the occasional opening and shutting of a door and the continuous struggle of Silas Trott's raucous breathing.

Suddenly they were conscious that the latter sound had ceased. They stared at once another with frightened, questioning eyes and dared not put into words the thought that was in all their minds. Jean, sitting on the floor, crept close to Lois and buried her face in her older sister's lap. And Tim, sitting nearby, reached out and clasped the hand of Lois in a warm and comforting grip. All three positively jumped, as the door opened and the doctor entered, followed by a tearful Ellen, openly wiping her eyes on her apron. The doctor gave one understanding glance at the huddled trio and spoke:

"I've come to bring you some good news, folks! We think Mr. Trott has turned the corner and is going to live!" He walked over to the cheerful blaze and warmed his hands, then sank wearily into a chair nearby and waited till the girls' and Ellen's sobs of relief and sheer joy had quieted a bit. Then he went on:

"Yes, the fever's gone down and he's breathing more easily and has dropped off into a natural sleep for the first time since his illness began. He has a magnificent constitution. It was the one thing in his favor. There's a chance that there may be a relapse, of course, but if all goes as it promises now, Mr. Trott will recover." There was an audible sigh of heartfelt relief from every one of his hearers.

"But," he went on after a moment, "there's one thing I want to warn you all about. Though he may recover from this illness, Mr. Trott's health is never going to be quite the same again. He's not a young man, and this violent pneumonia has been a terrible strain on his heart. That heart's never going to be what it was, and he's got to settle down to favoring it as he would a sick baby. No more lifting and tugging at heavy furniture, no more going out in all sorts of weather—in fact, no more *anything* that he's been used to doing. And I don't know how he's going to take it, for I understand he's always been a pretty active man. But you people who care for him have just got to see to it that he cuts out all that sort of thing. It won't be easy, once he gets on his feet again. But I've warned you! I won't be responsible for the consequences if he breaks this rule—*one single time!*"

They all nodded understandingly, and Ellen was heard to mutter: "The saints save us, for I don't know how we're going to manage him! But praise be to Heaven, he's going to get well—anyhow!"

11. A New Regime

SILAS TROTT had "turned the corner." But it was early indicated that his recovery was to be a slow and heartbreakingly tedious affair. After the crisis was past and the long, uphill journey back to strength and more normal conditions had begun, trouble broke out between Miss Jenks and Ellen, just as Lois had feared. And it fell to her unhappy lot to have to act as peacemaker between them, in which role she was frequently quite unsuccessful. At last Ellen begged the doctor to send the nurse away and let *her* take charge of the patient, as she had had much unofficial experience in that line. And this the doctor was happy to do, both because he was weary of Miss Jenks's complaints and because she was needed in other quarters. So, to the secret joy of the whole household, the day came when she had packed her things and was ready to depart. They deeply appreciated what she had done in their great emergency, but she was a difficult person to live with, particularly in this rather unusual establishment.

Just before she left, minus her starched white uniform and unfamiliar in her street-dress, coat, and hat, she took Lois aside in the living room and made a curious statement. She began by asking a question.

"This is quite out of order," conceded Miss Jenks, "but I'd like to ask you something. There isn't anything wrong with your uncle's mind—under normal conditions—is there?"

"Heavens, *no!*" exclaimed Lois. "Why—why do you ask?"

"Well," acknowledged the nurse, "of course people say all sorts of crazy things when they're delirious, and nurses don't pay much attention to them. But Mr. Trott kept repeating one thing over and over when he was out of his head, and after a while I couldn't help but take notice of it. It must be something that's been on his mind normally, because when the fever left him and he came to himself he must have realized he'd been saying some queer things. He asked me several times if he'd said anything special when he was out of his head—and what it was. Of course I wouldn't think of repeating it to him. That would only upset him and might cause his fever to rise again. So I just soothed him down and told him he'd mumbled a good deal but that I hadn't had any time to pay attention to that—I was too busy taking care of him. And that sort of satisfied him."

"But what *was* it he said?" demanded Lois, thoroughly bewildered.

"He kept calling out, *'I know it—I know it's somewhere. I have the Count's written word for it. I'll find it if it takes the rest of my life!'* Under the circumstances," ended Miss Jenks, looking about at her surroundings with her peculiarly critical glance, "you'll have to admit that it sounds very strange. I'd watch him in the future rather carefully, to see whether his—er—mind's slipping. That's all!"

And with that Miss Jenks took her departure, superciliously sniffing at the Colemans' car, which Zeph had borrowed to take her on the long drive to her train. And Lois was left with one more baffling surmise to add to the accumulation piling up since her entry into Silas Trott's household.

Then had begun the work of reorganizing the establishment along new and unfamiliar lines. It was quite appalling, how many puzzling situations had to be met. Lois and Ellen had to cope with them all, aided by Tim, when he was at home, for they speedily realized that Silas Trott must not be disturbed by having any of them referred to himself, at least for a long time to come. Added to that, Silas showed himself curiously apathetic now where most of his former normal occupations were concerned. It seemed as if the fever had burned out of him all the vigor and vitality he once possessed and had left him weak and empty and content merely to lie in bed, thinking about nothing. When the time came that he was allowed to sit up in a chair and move out into the living room, he continued to be gentle and indifferent, taking only a casual interest in household affairs, dozing all day over some old book or idly staring out of the window. The doctor thought this phase would pass after a while, but he said to Lois and Ellen:

"He'll never be what he was—never again. Something's left him. I don't know whether it's physical strength or some mental impetus that's missing. I had to tell him he'd never be able to hustle around physically the way he used to, because he had to know *that* from the beginning or he might some day get energetic and try to overdo. Perhaps that's the trouble. I don't know. Anyway, I couldn't take the risk of keeping him in ignorance about it. He'll get used to the idea after a while."

Meantime, the running of the household devolved upon Lois, Ellen, and Zeph. And one of the problems they found most difficult to deal with was the ever recurring matter of people arriving to buy from Silas's stock. They had been turning everyone away, and sometimes it proved very difficult to do so. At last one day, when Silas had been able to be wheeled out of his room (they had providentially discovered an old wheel chair among the furniture in one of the sheds!) and was sitting in a sunny window in the living room gazing out at the bare branches of a huge oak, Lois came to him and timidly put a question.

"I hate to bother you, Uncle Si, but we've been wondering if we couldn't do something about these people who come to buy things. We have been telling them you were ill and sending them away. And some of them act terribly disappointed. Is there any way that I could wait on them, perhaps? I could get an idea from you about the prices of things and Zeph could move the furniture out when necessary."

Silas Trott turned his listless gaze toward her and rested for the moment an affectionate hand on her arm.

"Thee must not worry about it, Lois," he murmured. "'Tis no great matter. Some day perhaps I shall be strong enough to take it up again. Till then—send them away. I do not very much care whether they buy or not."

"But, Uncle Si," she persisted, "forgive me for asking this—you see, I—I don't know anything about your—your money affairs. But—can you afford to lose all this business?"

He smiled wanly.

"I know what thee is thinking of, my dear, and I thank thee for being so considerate and thoughtful. I have sufficient—for all our needs—for the present. Do not think about that. I am enough trouble, as it is—practically a helpless invalid, making extra work for everybody. If it will take a burden from thee, put up a sign on the door, 'No More Furniture For Sale,' and let them make what they can of that!"

Lois had said no more at the time, fearing to upset him. And later she had a long talk with Tim, who had come home for a week end, and laid her troubles before him, as he understood the situation better than anyone else she knew. That Saturday was one of January's mild intervals, and they had strolled over the fields to the stream that ran in front of the little old brick house. In the warm sunshine, they seated themselves on the tiny veranda, and Tim occupied his idle hands by tossing pebbles into the clear brown depths of the running water. And Lois told him all that had transpired since he had left after the Christmas holidays.

Over the incident of Miss Jenks's strange remarks when she left, he pondered deeply.

"It's queer," he vouchsafed, at length, "but I always did think Uncle Si had some other purpose in his mind besides collecting old cast-off stuff and antiques, all these years. He has acted to me like a man who was after some secret thing, some special idea—and either used this old-furniture business to cover up his real purpose or else to help him attain it, if you know what I mean. And when he said, 'I'll find it if it takes the rest of my life,' he was saying exactly what he's always been trying to do. But what all this business of 'the Count's written word for it' can be, I haven't a notion. Who in conscience can the 'Count' be, anyhow? I never supposed Uncle Si had anything to do with the 'nobility.' Except—hey!—how's this? Suppose some 'Count' or other over in Europe has been getting him to keep an eye out for some antique—some special thing he happens to fancy? Get me?"

It was a new thought to Lois. "That *might* be it," she conceded. "Somehow it seems as likely as anything. But why keep it such a dark brown secret, though? I shouldn't think it would be anything to hide or be so mysterious about!"

"Well, you can't tell," argued Tim, more and more enthused with his own idea. "You know how these antique collectors are. They break their necks to get hold of something nobody else has—or get it first, before the other fellow can get even a smell of it! That's it—I'd be willing to bet!

It would explain a lot of the other peculiar things too."

"But it doesn't explain the locked room," objected Lois. Tim looked suddenly crestfallen.

"No, it doesn't," he had to admit. "I was going to say that was probably where he kept it. But then if he *had* it already, there wouldn't be any sense looking for it!"

"And besides that," added Lois, "there isn't anything *in* the room, anyhow. It's bare of everything except that oriental rug, and it isn't in the least likely that that's it. So there you are!"

"By the way, did he ever ask for his keys—or say anything about that scrap of paper?" inquired Tim.

"I took his keys to him, after he'd gotten a bit better, and told him I had been keeping them for him and would now put them back in his bureau drawer," said Lois. "He thanked me and said to leave them there. We've had to borrow them once in a while, when we wanted to get something for him out of the storage barns—like his wheel chair. I didn't know quite what to do about the paper. I hated to hand it to him because it might upset him. So I just slipped it in under the keys in the drawer. The other day when I was getting him a handkerchief out of that drawer, I noticed that the paper was gone. He is able to get around his room a little by himself now, so I imagine he has put the paper away or more likely destroyed it. We've never mentioned the subject—and probably never will."

"Awfully queer thing, that whole business!" mused Tim. "I wonder if we'll ever have an explanation of it all? If Uncle Si has—"

He got no farther. Suddenly they were both stunned to hear, from inside the closed and apparently empty little house, the sound of a loud crash and a smothered moan. Then all was silence again.

"Cripes!—did you hear *that?* gasped Tim.

Lois did not answer but pointed significantly to the shutter of a window opening on the veranda. The shutter, which had always hitherto been securely fastened, was now swinging open just an inch or two!

12. The Footprint

TIM SCRAMBLED impetuously to his feet. His intention was plain. He was about to rush to the window, tear open the shutter, and see what was wrong. But Lois, more cautious and timid, held him back.

"Oh—*don't!*" she breathed. "You can't tell who's in there. It might be someone who was desperate and would—would shoot—or something!" Tim shook her off and fiercely whispered:

"Someone's in there who hasn't any right to be! I'm going to see who it is. The quicker you act in a case like this, the better off you are. Let me go, Lois—and you stay right where you are!"

He shrugged off her detaining hand, ran over to the shutter and pulled it wide open. As he had suspected, the window was up and someone had very evidently made an entrance not so very long before. And in spite of Lois's horrified protest, he put one leg inside, ducked in his head, pulled in the other leg—and disappeared from view.

She stood where she was outside, in an absolute paralysis

of terror, waiting for—she dared not think what. At the very least, she expected to hear revolver shots or sounds of struggle from within, but no sound issued, though she waited what seemed to her an eternity. So long was it, indeed, that she was just about to set aside Tim's command and go in after him, when she saw to her unbounded relief that he had appeared again at the window. But instead of coming out he remained inside and beckoned to her.

"Can't find anybody!" he vouchsafed, when she had cautiously approached the window. "But someone's been in here all right. However they got away is a mystery I can't fathom. Want to slip in here and see what I've been looking at? You'll be surprised!"

"Do you—do you think I ought?" faltered Lois. "If Uncle Si keeps it locked up, perhaps I oughtn't."

"Oh, heck!" snorted Tim. "Don't be *too* fussy! Of course we wouldn't deliberately break in, but since somebody else has, there's not the slightest reason why we shouldn't look around and see if any damage has been done. And if you ask *me,* it's a darned good thing we happened to be around here this afternoon. We've certainly put a crimp in *somebody's* house-breaking plans!"

Needing no further persuasion, Lois signified that she would follow him, but asked, peering into the window:

"Isn't it awfully dark in there? I mean the rest of the house. I didn't bring any flashlight, and I don't suppose you did either. How can we see our way around?"

"I have some matches," answered Tim, "and it isn't as dark as you think. Hurry up! I don't want anyone to come sneaking back, perhaps, and catch us in here. Rather be on the outside looking in, in *that* case!"

He laughed nervously and helped Lois in over the windowsill. And at last she stood in the little red brick house that had been such a mystery to her! What she saw took her breath away, as it had taken Tim's when he had first entered.

They had both supposed it to be entirely empty. It was not. On the contrary, Lois found herself standing in a room illuminated dimly by the light admitted by one open shutter, but showing itself furnished almost to the last detail in the most utterly charming early American fashion! A huge, winged grandfather's chair in quaint chintz and an English Windsor chair flanked the open fireplace, above whose carved white-painted mantel hung a gilt girandole. Against one wall stood a Duncan Phyfe mahogany sofa upholstered in faded but rich brocade. Against another stood a handsome dark mahogany highboy with wing-shaped brass escutcheons and handles. There was a corner cabinet with a marvelous arched shell effect at the top, a small "pie-crust"-edged table, and another of mahogany drop-leaf variety that had a gloss like satin. Two or three Chippendale chairs and an unusual hooked rug on the painted floor completed the furnishing, except for two fine old oil portraits and a couple of rare framed prints that hung on the walls.

Tim watched Lois staring about and striving to express her unutterable astonishment, and grinned:

"What did I tell you! Some little exhibition of antiques—what?"

"Why—I—I feel as if I were in a part of the American Wing in the New York Museum of Art!" gasped Lois. "How did it ever get like this? Is all the rest of the house the same?"

"Come and see," said Tim for answer. "Only look out where you step. I've only a few matches to light us, and it's pitch dark in the rest of the place." He led the way into the tiny hall, unfurnished except for a rare print or two on the walls. A spindle-railed stair of quaint design mounted to the upper floor, but he led the way to the rear, opening a door and striking a fresh match as he did so. Peering in over his shoulder, Lois beheld a combination dining room and kitchen all done in early American maple. While the match flared, her eye caught the charming array of blue Delft dishes ranged on another maple corner cupboard, the pewter and copper bowls and utensils, the ancient fireplace with the cranes and pothooks of Colonial days, the beautifully braided rag rugs on the floor. Then the match went out.

"It just seems too marvelous to be true!" she murmured. "Is there anything upstairs?"

"Follow me!" commanded Tim. "We'll leave the front-room door open so that it will light the hall and save us a match or two." And he ran lightly up the stairs, Lois following close behind.

"There are three bedrooms up here," he informed her, as they reached the upper landing, which was square in shape, with three doors opening from it. "The biggest one is in the front, the two smaller ones at the back. They're all furnished in the same type as downstairs, and I haven't enough matches left to let you take more than a quick peek at each one. So don't linger over them, for there's something else I want to show you."

He lighted a match in each doorway, and Lois had just a brief glimpse of three bedrooms, quaintly done in rare four-posters, heavy bureaus of exquisite cabinet work, oval framed mirrors, patchwork quilts, and, in the front room, over the mantel, a large portrait, in oils, of a lovely young girl with a hauntingly attractive face and dark hair wound in a simple knot at her neck. Lois would have liked to examine this portait more closely, but the match went out and Tim refused to sacrifice another to the purpose.

"I've something else to show you," he warned, "and I've only two matches left. So come ahead downstairs. Something looks mighty queer about this whole affair." He closed the door of the front bedroom, but before going downstairs again he lit another match and for Lois's benefit illuminated the little square upper hall. There was nothing whatever in it except a round braided rug and, against one wall, a quaint, rush-bottom ladder-back chair which probably had first seen the light in some early Colonial kitchen.

"Do you see that chair?" questioned Tim, pointing at it while the match burned down in his fingers. Lois nodded. "Well, when I came up here first, alone, that chair was lying on its side in the middle of the hall. I had to take it up and put it where it is now before I could get by!"

"Then—then—" faltered Lois, and Tim interrupted:

"Yes, you've guessed it!—that's what made the crash we heard. But who did the groaning, or where they got to, is beyond me!"

"Oh, let's get away from here!" breathed Lois, grabbing his arm and pulling him toward the staircase. "It just scares me to pieces to think some desperate person may be around—and we trapped in here and unarmed!" Tim laughed at her fears.

"You weren't very frightened when you were looking about a minute ago!" he jeered. "You wanted to stay longer then."

"Well, it all surprised me so—the inside of this house—that I sort of forgot what had happened at first," Lois excused herself. "But I want to go out—right away—and get out of this—this *trap!*"

"Just a minute—till I use up my last match," he temporized, and, lighting it, he examined, while it burned, the seat of the chair and the floor around it. Then that match too burned out, and they were left with only the faint light from the open downstairs door to guide them back to the lower front room.

"We'll have to get out the window again, for the front door's locked.

"I'll fix the shutter as securely as I can, till I can come back with a padlock to make it more secure."

"Shall we tell Uncle Si about this?" asked Lois doubtfully. "I suppose we should."

"Better not!" counseled Tim. "He's still in a pretty weak condition, and it might upset him a lot to hear about this. You can't tell what it might do to him in the state he's in. We'll just have to take the responsibility of it ourselves. I'll padlock or nail up this shutter and try to keep an eye on the place as long as I'm here. And when I have to go back, I believe I'll just get old Gedney Stevens to take over the job. You know, he's town constable as well as postmaster, and he knows how to mind his own business. And another thing—he's always thought so much of Uncle Si that he'd sit up nights with a shotgun to watch this place if he thought anyone was trying to get funny with his friend Silas Trott's property!"

"But, Tim," said Lois suddenly, after they had crawled out of the window and were standing on the little porch again, "*what* can have become of the person who knocked over the chair and made that groaning sound? He—or she —must have gotten away *somewhere*—and they certainly didn't come out of that window!"

"That's what gets me," admitted Tim. "The way I figured it out, someone got in here through the downstairs window and was prowling around when they heard us talking down on the porch and suddenly decided they'd better beat it. In going through the upper hall (probably without a light) they knocked over that chair and perhaps gave themselves a bad bruise, which caused the groan. Then they hustled down and out somehow, though where there was a cranny to get through beats me. I thought first that maybe they might be hiding somewhere in a closet or something. And I opened every door I could find—but nothing doing."

"There's a cellar, isn't there?" suggested Lois. "I never knew of a brick house that hadn't one—of some kind."

"Let's walk around the place and see," said Tim. "I want to see, anyway, if there are any traces outside of whoever got in here. There *is* a cellar, too. But no opening to it from inside. I thought of that at first, and looked. But there was no doorway to any stairs leading down. Now that I think of it, there's an outside cellar door at the back—the kind that opens in a slanting way, you know. But that wouldn't do the person that was inside the house any good."

They walked all the way around the house, staring at every inch of ground for a trace of the intruder, but there was none. Grass ages old and knee high grew close to the sides of the house where it was not overgrown with bushes, and showed no telltale signs. At the rear, under the closely shuttered kitchen windows, was a slanting cellar door, strongly padlocked and showing no indication of having been tampered with. The weeds and bushes had grown rather close about the back of the house, and all signs of paths or walks around it had long since disappeared. They turned to go round to the front, at last, by way of the opposite side from which they had come, finding, in the main, the same condition on that side as on the other. Suddenly, in passing a slightly depressed and muddy bit of open ground, Tim bent down with a low, surprised whistle.

"Look here!" he cried to Lois. "Old man Friday's been around, all right. Look at that!" He pointed to a solitary footprint, well planted in the moist mud and so distinct that even the hollow places in the rubber heels were visible.

"It's a *man's!*" exclaimed Lois. "Are you sure it isn't *yours,* Tim?" For answer he planted his own foot in an open space nearby and lifted it again. The impression was entirely different, being that of a rubber-soled and -heeled sport sneaker, crisscrossed over the sole in a pattern as dissimilar as possible from the plain impression of the other sole. "Besides, I haven't been around this side till now," added Tim, as if extra confirmation were needed.

"No, this is the guy that's been sneaking about. And just recently, too, for that impression was made sometime today. This looks pretty bad. I think I'll go right over and report the thing to old Gedney and get him on the job!"

13. Jean Tries an Experiment—With Some Surprising Results

THERE HAD been a marked change in Jean since the first days of Silas Trott's illness. Before that time, her attitude toward him had been one of polite but rather evident indifference. Insofar as her twelve-year outlook on life permitted, she was grateful to him for what he had done for herself and Lois, but that was about all He had meant to her little more than the person in whose house she was living and whose wishes had to be considered and obeyed. But of affection for him she had none, and in her forthright way did not pretend to any. Lois was different. She had sensed almost immediately Silas Trott's generous and affectionate attitude toward them, and it had won her own allegiance from the beginning.

Curiously enough, it had soon been noticed by both Lois and Ellen that Silas was unusually attracted by Jean. He would follow her with his eyes constantly, when she was anywhere in his vicinity, and was always more than ordinarily affectionate and indulgent toward her. It had rather worried Lois that Jean responded so little to his quite evident interest in her. But Jean was a law unto herself and Lois well knew that any remarks or expostulations about it to her would only drive her further from reciprocating his interest.

But after the critical days of his illness there had come a quite noticeable change in Jean's attitude toward her foster uncle. She seemed to lay herself out to be specially attentive and tender to him, sacrificing, when he had recovered sufficiently, much of her play time to sitting and reading to him or just amusing him with her chatter. And if Silas Trott took an interest in anything, at that period when he seemed to have so little interest in life, it was in Jean's presence and her lively and amusing way of talking to him. And Jean was with him more than she would normally have been, of late, because she had had a rather serious spat with Sandy, and for several days he had gone off to play baseball with some of the boys in the town, instead of romping with her. She felt his desertion rather keenly, and Silas commented on it one afternoon as she sat doing her homework in the living room where he now spent so much time in his wheel chair.

"Thee rather misses Sandy, I reckon!" he had remarked to her as she sat frowning over a complicated problem in fractions. "What seems to be the trouble between you?"

"He's a horrid boy!" declared Jean, forsaking her arithmetic and coming to sit beside him on a footstool. "He always wants to be leader in everything—and never gives me a chance at all."

"That's the boy of it!" smiled Silas. "He will get over it some day—but I know it is hard to put up with. But I know, too, thee is rather lonely."

"I'm *not!*" declared Jean stoutly. "I wouldn't think of being lonely for that little *object!* And, besides, I like it a great deal better to be with you. You know such a lot of interesting things—and you don't treat me as if I were no account at all—like most grownups do!"

"Thee is very kind to say so, Jean," returned Silas, somewhat flattered by her attitude, "but thee must find it rather boring—the company of a sick old man who has to be constantly waited on. Yet it is very pleasant to have thee about!" Jean leaned her head against his knee, and he laid his hand shyly on her dark curls. Suddenly she felt impelled to ease her mind of something that had been bothering it for quite a while past. In fact, at times when she had allowed herself to think of it, she had really been quite conscience-stricken. She suddenly determined that this was the time to confess.

"I want to tell you something, Uncle Si," she began, wheeling round so that she could face him. "Before you got sick, I did something one day that I'm afraid you wouldn't like. But while I was doing it, I found out something I think you ought to know, too." She hesitated and waited to see the effect of this remark on Silas Trott. She had determined that if he acted annoyed, or was inclined to be unpleasant about it, she would tell him as little as possible about the matter and let it go at that. Silas looked down at her quizzically. Smiling a little, he said:

"They say that 'open confession is good for the soul,' and thee need not be afraid to tell me anything, my dear!"

"Well, you know the little red brick house," went on Jean, "the one that's all shut and locked up?" Silas nodded, a slightly startled expression dawning in his eyes. "I did something that was awfully wrong, I suppose," Jean continued in a low voice. "I've always been awfully curious about that house 'cause it *was* all closed tight and no one lived there. I asked Mrs. Coleman, one day, who owned it, and she said you did, but that she thought it was empty. So once, near Christmas, when no one was around one afternoon, I just decided I'd go over there and explore a bit. I thought if you owned that it couldn't be any harm my doing it, 'cause it would be just like our own home too. I couldn't find any way to get in downstairs, so I saw that rose trellis up the side of the veranda and climbed up to the veranda roof on that. I nearly fell off it twice," she added impishly.

"But I got up all right at last and tried the shutters to see if any one was loose. One window was all tight. But on the other one, the shutter just came loose when I pulled at it, and I found that the nail it was fastened to inside had rusted away. And when I had the shutters open, I—I just couldn't help but peek in. And—and what I saw surprised me a lot, 'cause I'd thought it was empty. Then it was raining hard, and I shut the shutters as well as I could and shinnied down the post of the porch. I meant to go there again sometime, but I never did, and after that you got so sick, and I felt awfully bad about what I'd done. And I hope you'll forgive me, Uncle Si!" She stopped and looked at him appealingly, and was rather amazed at the troubled expression in his eyes. He did not reply for a moment, while Jean waited in suspense, thinking he was probably greatly annoyed with her. Finally he said:

"I like the honesty with which thee has told me this, Jean. And as the spying was very natural and innocent, I cannot be displeased with thee. In fact, I am really very glad thee did it, because thee has discovered a very serious situation that might cause much trouble, as I seldom go over there. And as things are now, I could not if I wished. Now, attend to me carefully, and try to follow my orders, for I want thee to help me get this situation with the shutter rectified without bothering anyone else about it. It is too late to attend to the matter today, but tomorrow afternoon I would like thee to take a hammer and nails and go over there. I will give thee the key to the house from my key ring, so there need be no more climbing of porches! And thee must take the flashlight with thee. When thee gets in, go upstairs and do the best thee can to supplement that rusty nail with a fresh one. Then thee might go about to all the other shutters and see if they are secure. It will greatly ease my mind to know that this is done. Can thee do it for me?"

"Oh, Uncle Si! I'll just be crazy to do it!" exclaimed Jean, keenly thrilled over the new adventure. Then a sudden thought struck her. She wanted to ask him why he didn't allow Zeph to do it—or Tim. She wanted to ask him the meaning of what she had seen through the window— the bedroom all furnished in the style of an early day— when the house was supposed to be empty. She wanted to ask him a number of things, but just at that moment Ellen entered the room with a glass of milk and some medicine and a plate of fresh cookies for Mr. Trott.

"Ye'll have to go down to the store for me, Tiny," she had announced, "and get me some poultry seasoning and another loaf of bread. I can't leave me dinner on the stove, and I need the seasoning at oncet." And Jean knew that the time for any further confidences with Uncle Si was over, for when she came back Ellen would be setting the table, and the family would all be about. So she gave Silas Trott an understanding nod, seized a handful of cookies, and sallied out on the errand, marveling at the luck which had befallen her in being permitted lawfully to enter the little red brick house.

The next afternoon, the coast being clear (which meant that Ellen was busy in the kitchen and Lois out somewhere with Tim), she approached Silas Trott and asked for the key to the little red house.

"I have the hammer and nails," she informed him. "I got them from Zeph, out in the woodshed. He thinks I want them for a hut Sandy and I were building out in the yard. Everyone is busy or off somewhere, so I think this is a good time to get that job done."

Silas, smiling, handed her the key, which he had extracted from his ring, and bade her be sure and take her flashlight, as she would find it dark in the house with all the shutters closed. She was greatly tempted to stop and talk with him awhile about the questions that puzzled her, but realized that he would be anxious for her to get the thing accomplished. And if she lingered too long, Ellen might capture her and put her to work in the kitchen. So with a gay smile to him, she fled noiselessly out through the front door, skirting around the side of the house farthest from the kitchen windows, and reached the little brick house by a roundabout route.

That she was entering this closed and mysterious little house with a perfectly lawful key to its front door detracted no whit from the thrill Jean experienced—in fact, it added to it. And when she had pushed open the door and stood in the musty little hall, she turned on her flashlight and stared about her with an indrawn breath of exhilaration. But first she carefully locked the door on the inside, as Silas had bidden her to remember, because, as he had said, a door left open or unlocked was always a temptation to a possible stranger strolling by. This done, she pushed open the door of the front room and entered, flashing her light before her as she went.

"Might as well look at these shutters right at the start," she told herself. But in reality her curiosity to see what was to be seen on the lower floor immediately was the real impulse for this move! And for several moments she stood, flashing her flashlight hither and yon, almost gasping at the quaint and unexpected beauty of its furnishings.

"Golly!" she muttered aloud. "I wonder why Uncle Si furnished it like this. And why doesn't he want anyone to see it or know about it? I call this one *grand* mystery!" But at length she had seen her fill, and turned her attention to the shutter fastenings, first raising the windows to get at them. She found them intact, so, shutting the windows, she hurried through the hall into the room at the rear. Here she spent another period of inspection and wonder, examined the shutters, found them quite as they should be, and scampered upstairs to complete her tour of inspection.

The two smaller rooms at the back being closer to the head of the stairs, she entered them first and repeated the performance. Plainly, however, there was no shutter save the one she had originally discovered that needed any attention, so she entered the front room. It looked as she had seen it the first time, when she had peered in the window, except that now she was in a position to observe many things that did not come within her range of vision that day. Before the portrait of the lady over the mantel she paused a long time, studying it intently.

"Funny!" she thought aloud. "I wonder who she is. She's awfully pretty, specially in that old-timey sort of dress. I bet it's just some picture Uncle Si picked up at one of those auctions and hung it here 'cause it looks nice. But I like it— I like it a lot—and I don't know why!" Suddenly she noticed that the flashlight was becoming very weak.

"Oh, heck!" she thought distractedly. "The batteries are giving out! I ought to have got some new ones. If they die on me and leave me in the dark, it'll be just too bad!"

She rushed over to the windows, examined them both, and found the shutter she had pulled out on that first visit the only one that needed attention. So, laying her flashlight along the sill where it would cast the most light, she hurriedly began to extract what was left of the old, rusty nail-fastening and supplied a new one. And as she was naturally handy with tools, this was not as great a task as it might have been for a less experienced person. In three minutes she had hammered home the new nail, fastened the shutter securely, and closed the window. Then she drew a long breath and prepared to review the quaint little house again, more at her leisure, and for as long as her dwindling flashlight would hold out.

Inevitably the portrait of the beautiful woman of long ago drew her. She stood gazing at it in the feeble and waning light, when suddenly a faint but unmistakable sound from below stiffened her to acute attention. There was a dull, grating sound, a sudden snap, and then silence. Jean's heart positively stood still, waiting to hear what would follow. Nothing did.

"I guess it was just the old house snapping and cracking the way they sometimes do," she whispered to herself. "It *couldn't* have been anything else!" She breathed more freely again, but somehow the enthusiasm for prowling about the little house had waned, and she hastily determined that it was time to go back. She had just laid her hand on the knob of the door, when she was frozen into terror again. There were soft but distinct sounds of footsteps, tiptoeing up the stairs!

Jean was only twelve, but she was very keen, and she knew that she was caught in a trap in this dark house, with someone who had no business there coming steadily up the stairs toward her. Flight was impossible. And to meet the intruder face to face would be equally dangerous. There seemed to the distracted child but one other course open to her—to *hide,* as speedily as possible and in this same room where she stood.

With one sweep of her flashlight she covered the room, seeking wildly a retreat—any retreat—where she could crawl and conceal herself. There was a door, almost alongside the one that opened into the hall. She had explored its possibilities when she first came into the room. It gave on a closet—an empty one—and she knew that concealment in it now would be worse than useless. Discovery would be immediate. The steps were coming closer. There *must* be some other place!

There was. Around the bottom of the huge four-poster bed there hung a deep valance of some faded, ancient material. Jean turned out her flashlight, stuffed it in her pocket, clutched her hammer in her hand as a last weapon of defense in case she needed it, and dived under the bed!

14. Three Keep Their Own Council

DARKNESS. DUST. The musty odor of old furniture and draperies. The stifling inability to draw a free breath. The cold, paralyzing terror. And the furtive steps drawing nearer and nearer!

Close to the wall Jean crouched, flattened against it near the head of the big four-poster, clutching her hammer in her hand. The unknown person was now advancing along the little hall, had gently opened the door, and had halted in the room itself. There was some kind of faint illumination. Jean could see it through the folds of the valance that surrounded the bed. She judged it to be a candle, as it was too dim for a flashlight and too steady for a match.

The light began to move about the room, and there was a clicking sound which Jean took to be the opening and shutting of the closet door. Then it came to a halt near the mantel, for what purpose Jean could not determine, unless to allow a glimpse at the portrait over the fireplace. After that it hovered uncertainly before the windows and moved over toward the bed. It was in this moment that the shuddering child, crouched behind the valance, gave herself up for lost.

But after a moment the light seemed to move away, and presently Jean realized that it was leaving the room. The relief was almost too great to be borne in silence. She felt like screaming and shouting with delight. But she realized, too, that the danger was by no means over. The light had vanished, leaving the door partly open, and it took no great effort of imagination to picture that the intruder was no doubt investigating the two smaller rooms at the rear. As she thought it likely that the lower rooms would come last, since they had plainly not been examined when the prowler first got in (and how did he get in, anyway? she mused), she might have a chance to slip out and away, even if she had to open a shutter and climb down the porch pillar again, before he should come upstairs once more. Perhaps she might do that right now, while he was occupied at the back of the house! But no. He had left the door partly open and might spy her in the act of opening the shutter. Better wait for him to go downstairs.

She had settled herself for another uncertain interval, feeling fairly certain that he *would* go downstairs next, after the rear rooms had been examined. (Who *was* the intruder and what was he looking for, anyway? Now that her extreme terror had somewhat passed, she felt she would like to get a glimpse of him.) True to her surmise, after a time she heard the footsteps emerge from a back room and hesitate, apparently, at the head of the stairs. Surely he was now going down, and she would have a chance to escape by way of the window. With all the shutters and the door closed, he could not possibly see her. And she had determined that she would watch outside, from some hidden nook, and spy on him as he came out and report him later to the proper authorities. Such trespassing should not go unpunished!

She had just reached this laudable determination, when an entirely unexpected event happened. The steps halted at the top of the stairway for a long and (for Jean) suspense-filled moment. Then, to her complete amazement, instead of going on down, the steps came hurrying back along the hall, halted apparently in the middle of it, and something mysterious went on that Jean could neither imagine nor picture. Suddenly she was stunned to hear a sharp crash, as of some falling piece of furniture, a low groan, and then all was silence.

She lay where she was, shuddering anew, wondering what could have happened and where the intruder was now. She would have given much to raise the side of the valance next to the door and peep out, but she sensed that this would be too utterly dangerous. For all she knew, he might be standing right in the room—or near the door. She resolved to lie where she was, quietly, for a long while, till she heard no more sounds, before she so much as dared to put her head out from under that shielding valance. But she was soon to have another surprise.

She was presently aware that there were more footsteps on the stairs—not furtive ones, this time, but hurrying—taking two steps at a clip. Matches were scratched as if the way were being intermittently lighted by them. Just for an instant, a match was struck in the doorway, and someone in its light was staring all about, even opened and closed the closet door. Then all was darkness again and the hurrying footsteps went toward the back of the hall, where undoubtedly they disappeared into the rear bedrooms, then downstairs again.

"Now who in the world can *that be?*" thought Jean, distractedly. "It certainly wasn't the first one—and where has *he* got to? Maybe it's someone who's with the first one, that got here later and is trying to find him. What shall I do now? Better wait awhile longer, I guess." She had just settled down to another indefinite period in her stifling, dusty retreat, when she was again electrified by hearing footsteps down below—this time, undoubtedly made by more than a pair of feet—she could not tell accurately how many. And besides that there were whispered interchanges of remarks.

After an interval the steps could be heard ascending the stairs and doors were opened and more matches scratched. There were certainly two people—possibly more. And they were undoubtedly examining each room by striking matches and observing what they could by the light of each. In the doorway of the one where she was, they stopped, did not enter, but merely paused a moment, lit a match or two, whispered some remarks she could not catch, closed the door, and lingered awhile, striking more matches in the little hall. Then they trailed downstairs again and evidently left the house by whatever entrance they had come in. And once more all was silence.

Jean lay in her dark and dusty retreat, thoroughly bewildered by this new turn of affairs. What did it all mean? Who was the first intruder—and where had he disappeared? Who was the second? Who were the others and where were they all now? Dared she yet come out of her hiding place and make her escape to safety? Or would she be caught while still in the house? It was a desperately uncertain situation. And there was something about that earlier crash and moan that would not be explained by any theory she could imagine. So she continued to lie motionless for what seemed an interminable interval.

How long she remained thus she did not know for she had no watch with her and would scarcely have dared to turn on her flashlight and consult it if she had. But when the silence had continued so long that she felt sure every one of the invaders must by now be gone from the premises, she turned on the waning light of her flashlight and slid noiselessly out of her retreat. Then came the question: should she go out by way of the stairs and the front door, or should she open a window and shutter of the room she was in and try once more the adventure of sliding down by means of a porch pillar?

She opened the bedroom door a mere crevice and peered anxiously into the hall. Silence and darkness there and not a sound throughout the house. But at that moment a rather terrifying thing happened. Her flashlight went out completely, nor would any manipulating of the button revive it. And she knew then that her earlier fears about the batteries were verified. They had "gone dead" irretrievably! And she was left to the mercy of the dark.

Wildly she tried to decide what was best to do under this new condition. If any one of the unknown were perhaps left in the house, it might be better to make a dash for the window and escape into the open by that quicker route. On the other hand, if he were waiting about in hiding outside, and saw her making her exit by way of the porch pillar, he would be right on hand to capture her as she got to the ground—and she would be helpless to escape. Whereas, if she groped her way noiselessly down to the front door, unlocked it, let herself out and locked it after her, it seemed as if her chances to get out of the danger zone would be much better—provided always she encountered nothing to arrest her before she reached the door.

She decided finally on the door and began to grope her way through the dark hall, guided by the wall till she should get to the head of the stairs and the railing. Suddenly, in the dark, she stumbled against some obstacle which moved with a resounding noise, and her very heart stood in terror! It was the chair, sitting against the wall, as she instantly recognized, but whose presence she had quite forgotten. Paralyzed, she stood in her tracks, her heart pounding so audibly that she was sure it could be heard as plainly as had her collision with the chair.

But the silence continued unbroken. If anyone was in the house and had heard the racket, he gave no sign. Desperate with fear now, Jean stumbled to the stair head, grasped the rail and, holding to it, fled down the steps as if pursued by forty demons. She reached the bottom so much sooner than she had expected that she suddenly found herself in a heap on the floor of the lower hall, considerably bruised and shaken up by the impact. But she was on her feet in an instant, hurling herself at the front door, groping, fumbling with the key, searching madly for the keyhole, listening for furtive, pursuing footsteps on the stairs or in the lower rooms. But at last the key slid into the lock, turned, and she was out in the blessed open spaces, closing the door swiftly but silently behind her and locking it securely on the outside. Then, without another glance about her, terror still clinging to her like a wet garment that cannot be ripped away, she fled madly up the lane, out onto the broader road that formed the main street of Herbertstown, and found herself unscathed—and apparently even unseen—in the safe haven of Silas Trott's own front yard!

Once there, her unreasoning terror suddenly left her, and she sat down on the front steps to think it all over quietly. Her main problem was, what was to be done about the situation? Of only one thing was she certain. Silas Trott must *not* be told of the affair! In the weakened condition he was in, it might have the gravest results should she confide to him the terrifying and bewildering predicament in which she had found herself in the little red brick house that afternoon. She would report to him only that she had examined all the shutter fastenings and fixed the one that had been loose. And that would surely satisfy him. But, on the other hand, something ought to be done about the undoubted crowd of marauders that seemed to have found an entrance to the place. To whom, then, should she turn?

She reviewed the possibilities as they occurred to her. Ellen? Absolutely, *no!* Just the merest suggestion that she, Jean, had been in the precarious position of this afternoon, would automatically put a stop to all her future freedom, as far as the dictatorial Ellen was concerned. Lois? The same would apply to *her* knowing of the escapade, also. Tim was hand in glove with Lois and would undoubtedly report the whole affair immediately to her older sister. Mrs. Coleman would presumably do the same, and Sandy was too young to be of any real help. (Besides she was not even on speaking terms with him at present!) There remained only Zeph. And here, suddenly, was inspiration!

Of course, Zeph would be the proper and helpful one to speak to about it. The old colored man surely must know all about the little brick house and its surprising furnishings, to begin with. Who else could have been concerned in getting all those things in there and in order, if it had not been Zeph, working with Uncle Si! And Zeph, who hadn't very much to occupy his time these days when Uncle Si was so inactive, would have ample opportunity to watch the little house for another visit from the intruders. Yes, Zeph was by all odds the proper person. She would hunt him up immediately and tell him.

And with this plan in mind, she scrambled to her feet and darted round toward the back of the house.

15. Revelations by Gedney Stevens

LATE THAT same afternoon Lois and Tim together entered the post office and general store run by Gedney Stevens. The dark had fallen early, and the store was lighted somewhat dimly by three or four hanging kerosene lamps that did little more than irradiate the spot directly about where each was suspended. Out of habit, they both went straight to the corner where the mail boxes were, a series of pigeonholes on the wall guarded by a desk, and a little railing. Lois discovered nothing in her household box save a letter for Mr. Trott, which she stuffed in her coat pocket. The post-office department was being administered that evening by a young man of the village whom Gedney Stevens had taken and trained as clerk and general helper in the store. Gedney himself appeared to be nowhere about at the moment.

"Where's Mr. Stevens, Sergei?" asked Tim of the young Russian.

"He goes in the back there, to eat his supper," answered Sergei, pointing toward a door at the rear of the store. "He eats always early at night, so that when he comes back I go home for the rest of the evening."

"Well, we'll just knock and ask if he'll see us," commented Tim. "I have something I want to tell him, and I can't wait. I know he won't mind." He went to the rear of the store, Lois following at his heels, knocked at a closed door, and was bidden somewhat gruffly, to enter.

"It's only Lois and I, Mr. Stevens," he called, as he opened the door and closed it behind them. The room was Gedney

Stevens's living, dining, and sleeping room combined, the whole remainder of the building being given up to the needs of the store. But it was a large and surprisingly cozy apartment, curtained at its four windows with some bright, cheap cretonne, the bed concealed as a couch by day, with a gay cover to match the window draperies. There was a big warm rug on the floor, some well-filled bookshelves lining one wall, a roaring old cooking range connected with the chimney, and near it a little table at which Gedney was eating, an evening newspaper propped against the coffeepot to keep him company.

"Well! Howdy! Come in and have a seat—the two of ye!" exclaimed Gedney, rising from the table to welcome his guests. Lois thought, looking at him, that he was as typical a country storekeeper or farmer as she'd ever seen in the movies—with his bald head fringed with a sparse straggle of gray hair, his glasses down toward the tip of his nose when he was using them, or pushed up as now on his forehead where he had shoved them automatically at their entrance. His little, bright blue eyes twinkled knowingly as he greeted them, and Lois always wondered why there was a twinkle or a chuckle whenever she came into Gedney's vicinity—particularly if she was with Tim.

"Go right on with your supper, Mr. Stevens," begged Tim. "We oughtn't to have interrupted you, only it's something rather important." Gedney sat down again, buttered a slice of bread, and inquired:

"All right—guess I will if you don't mind. Sergei is waitin' to get home. What's eatin' you two at this time of night?"

"Kind of queer thing happened this afternoon," began Tim, "and we thought you ought to know about it." And he gave old Gedney an account of their experience in the little red brick house, omitting any special description of its interior decorations, as they rather imagined that Silas Trott had not told anyone of what had been done in the way of furnishing the little house since it had come into his possession. He ended by saying that they had thought it best not to worry Silas with the matter in his present condition, but had come straight to him, as constable of the town.

"Ye did right at that!" commented Gedney, scratching his head in perplexity over the singular affair. "But why didn't ye come straight to me when ye first got out? It was light then. And we might've caught whoever was in there, dead to rights. Now it's dark and they've probably beat it long ago."

"We did intend to," explained Tim, "and came back to do it. I wanted to get a hammer and nails too, or a lock of some kind to fasten that loose shutter at once. But unfortunately Mother saw me around the woodshed and begged me to come in and tinker a moment with her kitchen stove that had broken down in some way. She said it would only take a minute, so I tried it. But as a matter of fact, it took nearly an hour. Lois sat talking with her in the living room while I worked. When I got through it was nearly dark, and we hurried back there and made the shutter fast, so whoever got in won't get out *that* way again! And after, we came right over here."

Gedney poured himself a steaming cup of coffee and sat silent, thinking it over for two or three minutes. Then he cleared his throat loudly, took a very audible gulp of the hot coffee, and remarked:

"Well, ye did the best ye could—and as Shakespeare would say, 'angels could do no more'! And I'm glad ye didn't go tellin' Si about it. Sure do him up to know that place was bein' snooped around. He sets a heap by that place, Si does, ever since he bought it years ago. I dunno what he does with it—but I know he's spent a heap of time tinkerin' around in there nights when everyone thought he was to bed. I caught him one night comin' out of it—musta been near two in the mornin'!—and I says: 'I come durned near runnin' ye in for house-breakin', Si! Saw a light over here through the chink in the shutters movin' round, and I come over to lock up whoever was pokin' round this dump! Ye better git home to bed if ye don't want to get hauled in by the arm of the law!" Gedney chuckled softly at the memory. "And all he says to me was, 'Mind thine own affairs, Ged, and thee'll have all thee can handle. But thank thee, too, for keeping the place in mind.' He's like that, Si is. Greatest feller I ever knew fer keepin' his mouth shut about his own affairs. He's been the best friend I got around here for thirty years—and I reckon I'm the same to him—but on some things he's never opened his head to me since I knew him."

He seemed about to discontinue his remarks, but suddenly took them up again on another strain.

"But I know a good deal about Si's affairs that he don't *know* I know," he chuckled. "And I don't know's it's any breach of confidence to tell you 'bout 'em, seein' things are the way they are. Si's health ain't any too good yet, an' there's evidently some queer doin's going on hereabouts. And as you two know as much as you do, I think I'd best tell you what I *do* know. Then we can all form a sort of conspiracy to help Si, without him being bothered by any of it."

He stopped again and seemed to be thinking how to present the matter, while his two listeners held their breath in anticipation of what he should reveal. At last he seemed to have made up his mind, for he cleared his throat again and began:

"This here all happened years ago, and I never did know what it all meant, but I'm thinkin' it had some bearin' on the things that are goin' on right now. It was when that there little brick house had been standin' empty 'bout a year or two. The Jenkinses who'd always lived there 'way back from Revolution times, they'd moved off to Trenton or Newark or somewheres, so's the kids could go to high school an' the movies an' all that sort of thing. Anyway, a man an' his wife by name of Brown come an' hired it one time, an' said they was going to use it for fishing in trout season an' huntin' in the fall an' so on. Only I don't recollect seein' 'em doin' no huntin' or fishin' so long's they was here."

"Oh, yes, I remember Mother telling me something about them once," commented Tim. "They must have been a queer lot!"

"They was worse than that," added Gedney Stevens grimly. "From what I saw—and heard—I should say they was downright *criminal!* But it's what they did in regard to Silas Trott that I'm speaking of mainly. They came and went here at odd times. Never stayed very long, usually over a night or two, then lit out again. Si never let on he knew 'em, but I could see he was watchin' 'em like a cat all the time they was around. They never knowed I was a constable—never tell strangers that—it makes 'em easier to watch! But I was keepin' a weather eye on 'em all the time, 'cause I thought some of their actions was sort of suspicious. Fer one thing there never did seem no reason why they should be here. They was city folks—around Philadelphy way, I judged—and what they come here for had me beat.

"Well, one day whilst they was here, Si had been off all

day on one of his usual auction sprees, an' he didn't get back that night. I didn't know why first, 'cause it was unheard-of for him to stay away overnight, but I found out afterward he'd had a breakdown with the truck an' couldn't get it fixed till mornin'. Anyway, I got sort of worried about him as it got later an' later an' I took to watchin' his house to see whether he'd arrive. Just sort of stroll by there casual-like in the dark, once in a while. Well, you could eat me alive if one of them times I didn't spot a couple of dark figures sneaking around towards the back of his house! I sez to myself, 'Ged, this is where you get right on the job!' an' I started to sneak after 'em, sort of concealin' myself be-hind trees an' bushes, an' keepin' my gun hand ready fer the little persuader I carry in my hip pocket. They wasn't actually doin' anything I could nail 'em for—jest slippin' around the house eyein' the window shutters that Si always kept shut when he was away, an' measuring up the height of the second story—an' that sort of thing. I don't know whether they was plannin' to break in that night or not, but I thought after a while that the thing had gone far enough, so I let out one great big cough from behind the bushes where I was hidin'. My gosh!—ye never saw anything so funny in all yer life as the effect of that cough. I ain't stopped laughin' about it yet! They just turned tail an' beat it, like a pair of scared rabbits, round the house an' down the road till I lost sight of 'em in the dark. They was foxy enough not to go straight to the little brick house but kept right on goin' in the opposite direction. But it didn't fool me—no, *sir!* For I sneaked over to the woods on the opposite side of the crick just in front of that house, an' I watched there 'most an hour, an' presently I heard 'em come sneakin' back themselves and go into the house. And I knew then, durned well, who had been doin' the snoopin' around old

Si's place. But they never did see *me!*" He stopped to chuckle over the experience, finished his cup of coffee, and got up and went to the door to dismiss Sergei for the night.

"I can watch the store from here if I keep the door open," he explained to his two spellbound visitors. "Nobody comes in this time o' night anyhow. Everybody eatin'. But that ain't the end of my yarn—not by a jugful! I made up my mind I was goin' to keep my eye on them birds from then on. Didn't even let on to Si, because I thought it'd only worry him, an' meanwhile I could see that nothin' happened to his place while he was away. But let me tell you. I ran into something even funnier than what happened that night before I was through with it.

"Happened this way. After the good skeer they got, that precious pair disappeared for a spell from these parts and wasn't seen no more fer quite a while. But jest the same, I used to mosey over past that little red brick house every night, pretty late, jest in case they'd taken it into their heads to come into town after dark so's not to be seen. And sure 'nough, one night 'bout ten or eleven, there was a light in the place. It was a warm summer night, so the windows was open, and I hung around fairly close to hear what was goin' on. And you better believe I got an earful!"

"Oh, *what* did you hear?" breathed Lois involuntarily, as Gedney paused to spread another slice of bread and decorate it lavishly with sugar. "This is my dessert usually," he commented with a grin.

"I heard plenty," he went on, munching bread and sugar as he talked. "I wasn't near enough to catch everything, and I sorta had to piece things together, but they seemed to be quarrelin' about something. The woman was set on it, but the man had got cold feet, seemingly, and wanted to call it off. I heard the man say: 'Oh, what's the use? I'm for calling all this off and letting the poor devil alone. Hasn't he suffered enough?' And she let fly at him: 'You missed your chance years ago to make twice what you did on it. You have just as much right to it as he.' And he come back at her gloomy-like: 'I got what I asked—and you know where he spent five years. Besides, I'm dead certain he hasn't found it yet—if he ever does! It won't do the slightest good to search his place.'

"But that dame kept insistin': 'Maybe he *hasn't* it yet, but he's hot on the trail of it. And you know the Count never got it before he died. We might find out where old Trott keeps his records.'"

"The *Count!*" exclaimed Lois suddenly. "Oh, Tim, that must explain what the nurse was telling us!" And as Gedney looked at them curiously, she explained to him, under seal of strict secrecy, what Miss Jenks had revealed about the sick delirium of Silas, and her fears that his mind must be failing. Gedney shook his head.

"Si's mind's all right," he commented, "except that he's got somethin' on it that's been weighin' him down fer years, and all this has a big bit to do with it. But I'll go back to what I was tellin' ye. I didn't hear no more for a spell after that 'cause they got to lowerin' their voices 'bout what they talked of next. But jest before they quit, I heard her say: 'I've thought of a fine plan. We'll go to him and tell him *we've* discovered it ourselves and offer to sell it to him at a reasonable price jest to sort of make up for it all. And then maybe he'll loosen up and tell us what he's done and whether he's on the trail of it or not. We could kid him along quite a bit if he thinks we've really got it again.' And the man, he says: 'Might work—but you don't know that old Quaker skinflint the way I do. Anyhow we can try it. But let's go to bed now. It's late and I'm sick of the whole thing!'

"An' that was all I heard that night," ended Gedney Stevens. "I went home thinkin' it all over and wonderin' what I better tell Si about the job. Spent all next day thinkin' about it an' couldn't seem ter make up my mind. I'd got a bad splinter in my foot that mornin' and couldn't hardly hobble round. Si came in fer his mail, too, but a lot of others were in the store at the same time, so I let it go till evenin'. But by that time my foot was so bad I couldn't walk, an' I went to bed deciding I'd tell him next mornin' whether or no. But I was too late, after all. Found out next day that the pair had lit out durin' the night, and they ain't never been seen round these parts since. Short time after that, Si bought in the house, an' since then it's always been shut up. Guess they never did get a chance to pull the wool over his eyes the way they intended to!"

"Wait up!" suddenly exclaimed Tim. "I think I know the answer to that!" And he told old Gedney the story his mother had told him, and which he had already confided to Lois some weeks before, of the strange night interview she had once witnessed between Silas and the inhabitants of the little brick house.

"By heck, then!" cried Gedney, getting up and stamping about in his excitement at this revelation. "They *did* go over and try it on jest the very night when I was laid up and couldn't be on the job watchin' 'em! Ain't that the luck? And they probably threatened violence, too. Sounds like it from what Si said to 'em. Plucky old cuss, ain't he?"

At this moment Jean burst into the store, stared about her, and spied the trio through the open door of the back room. Dashing in, she exploded:

"Gee! I've been hunting all over the place for you two—

excuse me, Mr. Stevens!—but Ellen's had supper ready half an hour ago, and there's going to be waffles and they'll be all spoiled! And your mother's looking for you too, Tim. I was over there first! Whatever are you doing—staying out so long? You had both better come right home with me!"

They saw that further conference was out of the question, and guiltily realized that they had considerably delayed the usual evening meal hour, so they bade Gedney a hasty good-bye.

"That'll be all right," he remarked non-committally in parting. "I'll be tending to that matter and you needn't worry about it!"

"What did he mean?" demanded Jean when they were scurrying up the road homeward. "What'll he tend to?"

"That's something we can't explain," retorted Lois loftily and aggravatingly. "It happens to be our affair."

"Well, I've got affairs of *my* own," returned her small sister darkly, "and they're just as important as yours—maybe more so!"

In which case she spoke more truly than she knew!

16. Ellen Spends a Hectic Evening

ELLEN COULDN'T make out what was the matter with her family. It had seemed to her of late as if her whole world had gone completely "off the hooks," as she put it to herself!

Take Lois, for instance. She was jumpy and nervous, absent-minded when spoken to, never practiced on her piano any more, didn't eat enough to keep a bird alive, and spent most of the time mooning about, staring out of the windows in the direction of the little old red brick house down the lane. Ellen had questioned her intensively about how she felt, why she didn't take any interest in her meals, what was troubling her anyway. Lois had only answered vaguely that she was quite all right, felt perfectly well, and not to worry about her. Ellen had, for several days past, spent hours of time preparing all her beloved elder charge's favorite dishes, only to be rewarded by Lois sending away her food scarcely touched, or else making a strenuous but very obvious attempt at appearing to enjoy them. Ellen finally decided that she needed a tonic, and had Zeph drive her all the way to the nearest large town to purchase a bottle of cod-liver oil. Lois, who hated the stuff, had protested against it vainly, but finally shuddered over the doses, hoping by this means to quiet Ellen's apprehensions.

Then there was Jean. Noisy and rollicking as ever, at times, but with strange intervals of quiet, when she sat with Mr. Trott, reading or talking to him as she had never been known to before his illness, and with even stranger intervals of complete disappearance somewhere outdoors which she refused to comment upon. She was not with Sandy, Ellen knew, because the breach between the two children still held, and Jean was still withering in her scornful remarks about the red-headed youngster. "Now what was eatin' *her?*" thought Ellen distractedly. Her appetite at least hadn't failed, but she seemed to be around less frequently to snatch surreptitious handfuls of cookies between meals. *Something* had come over the child, and Ellen promised herself she'd find out what, or know the reason why!

Even Mr. Trott seemed to be affected by the general unrest. He still remained much of the time sunk in the apathy that had come upon him since his illness, but he too had curious fits of absorbed interest in watching something from his wheel chair in front of the window in the living room. Ellen couldn't imagine what it was, for from where he sat, nothing was within his focus of vision save one corner of the Coleman house and a glimpse of the little red brick one down the lane, through the vista of bare winter tree branches. And for the life of her she couldn't see where he could find a spark of interest in *that* sight! Once he had asked her anxiously if she ever noticed anyone around that little old house, and she had answered that she was usually at the back of the house and couldn't see it from the kitchen windows, so she had been totally unable to tell.

But most curious of all the strange goings-on in the establishment were the actions of Zeph. Now Zeph had always been an old man of settled and unchangeable habits. He ate with enormous appetite at regular meal hours. And outside of the work Silas had always required of him as his assistant in the furniture business, he had little else to do, especially since Ellen had come to take charge of the house and meals. Since Mr. Trott's illness he had had, it is true, far less strenuous work to do, and much more leisure time on his hands, but his general habits had remained practically unchanged—until lately. Now Ellen noticed that he was often late to his meals, or gulped them down hastily and hurried off when he was there on time. He had ceased being talkative and interested in her own comments on the world in general and their own lives in particular; was silent and uncommunicative, or answered her briefly and absently. And where he used to retire every night shortly after the evening meal to his little cabin in the rear of the yard, in which he spent long hours over the daily paper and some of the numerous old books he found lying about, he now went straight out after supper and away somewhere—she could not tell just where. But she knew it wasn't to his cabin, for the oil lamp she had usually seen burning till late was now seldom lit at all during the evening—or far into the night. Where he was spending his time, or what was taking him away every evening, she would have given much to know. She rather missed the long chats they had been wont to have in the evening, while he ate his supper and she washed the dishes. Altogether, Ellen felt that her world was very much awry.

On the night in question, she noticed the tense, abstracted air she was coming to dread, at the supper table, where a carefully prepared and truly delicious supper of creamed chicken and potatoes *au gratin,* for which she was famous, was going almost entirely to waste.

"Eat up that chicken, Tiny!" she commanded, as Jean pushed back her plate and prepared to be excused and to make an exit from the table.

"Don't want any more," retorted Jean, her eyes snapping with some unexplained and suppressed excitement.

"Certainly ye do!" remonstrated Ellen. "And besides that there's maple mousse for dessert." Jean visibly wavered.

"Thee'd better wait, Jean," advised Uncle Si. "What is thee in such a hurry about?" His question seemed to confuse the child even more than Ellen's commands.

"Oh, I just want to run over and see Sandy awhile," she remarked nonchalantly. And, seeing their rather surprised expression, went on:

"We made up our quarrel today. He 'pologized, and I said it would be all right with me, if he agreed that I could be leader every other time. So it's all okay again! But he's been kind of sick and his mother won't let him come over here tonight, so I said I'd run over there awhile and play games with him till bedtime. He's got a grand new jigsaw puzzle, too, that we're going to put together."

It had seemed a sufficient explanation, and they let her go—after the mousse had been duly consumed. Ellen extracted a promise that she would come back promptly at nine, and she dashed out directly after the last spoonful had disappeared.

Lois also seemed more than usually distrait that evening. She said that Tim was home for the week end and had promised to come over after supper and drive her to the nearest large town to the movies. But she seemed nervous and fidgety all through the meal and went out with Tim almost directly afterward. Mr. Trott told Ellen that he was feeling a bit tired that evening and would probably retire shortly after supper, which he did. And she repaired to the kitchen to wash the dishes and see that Zeph got his meal.

But Zeph did not come in at all, nor did he appear to be in his little shack. Ellen finished the dishes, put something aside on the stove to keep hot for him, in case he should appear later, got her mending basket and sat down in the warm kitchen to a perplexed and lonely evening.

"It's in the air!" she muttered to herself. "Somethin's goin' to happen. I feel it in me bones! The whole kit an' bilin' of 'em's acting that onnatural—I don't know what to make of it all!" She pulled one of Jean's short socks over her hand, examined a huge hole in the heel, and prepared to attack it. She rather loved these large and elaborate darning jobs. They helped to pass the time and acted as a sedative for bothersome thoughts. And a large, old-fashioned kitchen clock on the mantel (she had banished the other eight or ten!) ticked away the moments while she worked. And, what with the warmth and the quiet in the cozy kitchen, Ellen's eyelids began to droop. And after a while her work dropped in her lap, her head fell back against the chair, and she dozed, peacefully and uninterruptedly.

The booming of the clock on the mantel suddenly aroused her. Rubbing her eyes, she found, rather to her horror, that it was ten o'clock.

"Tiny must have come in and seen me nappin' and gone right up to bed without wakin' me," she thought, "but I'm sure Lois ain't in yet. She wouldn't've done that. I'd better be goin' upstairs to see." She heaved her great bulk out of her chair, went out into the hall, and slowly plodded up the stairs. But when she opened the door of the girls' room, a shock awaited her. Lois was not there, which she had expected, but—neither was Jean! Both beds were empty and the room was dark.

"The little spalpeen!" panted Ellen. "She's over there yet and she knows right well it's an hour past the time! Oh, my gorry! I s'pose I gotta get on me things and go over there to fetch her. She'll pay for this with no dessert fer a week!" So absorbed was she that she never looked down the hall toward another door, partly open, a faint light scarcely visible.

She lumbered heavily into her own room, found a large shawl which she draped over her head and round her shoulders, clumped downstairs again, and went out into the night. It was an exceedingly black night, cloudy and lowering, and as there were no street lights in Herbertstown, it was almost impossible to see ten feet ahead in the velvety darkness. But the lights from the living-room windows illuminated enough of the road for Ellen to get across to the Coleman house. As she mounted the porch steps, very cautiously feeling her way in the dark, she noticed to her dismay that a light in the living room was suddenly put out and the house was left in darkness. Hastily she thumped the brass knocker, and in another moment Mrs. Coleman had opened the door, peering out inquiringly into the darkness.

"It's only me—Ellen!" the visitor called out. "I've come to see why Tiny didn't come home at nine like I told her!"

"Why, Ellen," exclaimed Mrs. Coleman, "she *did!* I asked her when she was to go back, when she first came in, and she told me you had said nine. So I sent her off then and got Sandy to bed—he's been feeling sort of miserable the last two days—and then I came down and read awhile by myself. I was waiting for Tim to come in, but he and Lois haven't come back yet. I got so sleepy I finally decided not to wait for him, so I'd just put out the light and was going upstairs when you knocked. Where do you suppose Jean can be if she isn't home yet?"

Ellen didn't know, and her heart sank with undefined misgivings. But she somehow didn't want Mrs. Coleman to see that she was alarmed. So she temporized:

"Ye don't know that little divil yet, Mrs. Coleman! She probably come in and seen me nappin' by the fire and is hidin' somewheres jest to give me a scare when I woke up. She's played that trick more times than I can tell ye. But I'll fix her when I root her out, believe *me!*"

"Well, don't be too hard on her!" laughed Mrs. Coleman, completely reassured by Ellen's confident manner. "Remember, they're only young once, and they don't realize the trouble and worry these jokes of theirs cause us." She laughed again, bade Ellen good night and closed the door, while her visitor trudged down the steps and out into the darkness of the night once more.

But Ellen by no means completely believed what she had told Mrs. Coleman. There was a vague possibility of it, to be sure. Jean, had played a similar trick on her time and time again, chuckling in some safe hiding place, and watching Ellen hunt distractedly for her all over the house. But it was a trick the child had somewhat outgrown the last year or two, and she had never resorted to it since they had come to Herbertstown. Ellen felt a positive certainty that it was not the case in this instance, and she did not intend to go back and waste time searching through the house except as a last resort. She stood uncertainly in the dark road, striving to pierce the blackness about her and praying for some inspiration to guide her in her search for the missing youngster. She dared not go to Mr. Trott with the tale of Jean's absence. The shock might be most dangerous for him. And there was nobody else to whom she felt she could turn. Even Zeph was off on some unknown errand of his own. Oh, if only Lois and Tim would get back and help her in her perplexity! But they might not be back for another hour yet, and meantime she must do her own searching.

Where in all this black and benighted little town was she to turn first? Her only thought for the moment was that Jean might have slipped down to the general store to buy lollipops or chatter with old Gedney Stevens, with whom she'd struck up quite a friendship of late. But a glance down the street in that direction showed instantly that the store was dark and shut for the night. Where then?

Suddenly the idea of the little red brick house down the lane, and the intense interest the whole family seemed to have shown in it lately, flashed into Ellen's mind. Could it be possible that something had led Jean in that direction when she left the Coleman house? A cold chill of terror crept down Ellen's spine, and the moment the thought entered her mind, the certainty grew that there was indicated the direction in which she must search for the errant "Tiny." She gathered her shawl tighter about her, muttered a half-audible prayer for protection, and plunged down the pitch-black lane in the direction of the little red brick house.

17. Gedney Stevens Has an Idea

WHEN TIM called for Lois that evening to take her to the movies, his manner seemed unwontedly grave and subdued.

"What's the matter?" she had demanded, when they were out on the porch. "You act, Tim, as if you had the affairs of the nation on your mind!"

"Look here, Lois," he blurted, "are you so awfully keen on getting to the movies? Moorestown's quite a long drive, and—er—something rather important has come up."

"Why, no, of course not!" agreed Lois. "I like to go, as a rule, but some other time will do just as well. Why didn't you tell me at first? Does your mother want you to do something for her? Don't mind me. I've a grand book to read and we can go some other time."

"It isn't that," he replied uneasily. "The plain truth is, I had a talk with old Gedney late this afternoon when I first got home, and he told me some things that make me feel sort of anxious. He thinks there's something doing over at the little brick house."

"He *does?*" cried Lois incredulously. "I wonder why he hasn't told me anything about it, then. I go to the store every day, and he's never said a word."

"Probably didn't want to alarm you," said Tim. "He told me he's been watching every night this week, off and on, and he could swear that he's seen someone sneaking round the place each time. Never could spot him somehow, but he *knows* there's something going on. I half promised to join him tonight and see what's up and if we can catch the marauder red-handed, as it were! I told him I was booked to take you to the movies first and I'd try to get back early. But somehow I feel as if I ought to be on the job with him from the start. But I don't know what to do about *you!* If I leave you at home it'll look funny, after we'd fixed it all up to go. And if I leave you at Mother's it'll look queer to her and she'll be asking questions. What to do?"

"That's simple—take me with you!" pointed out Lois. "I'm not in the least afraid. I can tag along with you and Gedney and stay put, in some safe place where I can watch things, or you can leave me at Gedney's till you get back. Only I'd rather go with you. I'd be wild with suspense if I had to wait alone at Gedney's and wonder what was going on."

"Well, tell you what!" suggested Tim. "Come along to Gedney's now and we'll talk it over. We'll have to take the car or Mother will suspect something if she sees it around the house."

They scrambled into the Colemans' old sedan and whirled down the street, stopping abruptly in front of the general store and post office. Gedney was busy selling one of the Russian farmers a pair of overalls and looked up in some surprise when he saw them come in. He made no comment, however, and the two went over to inspect his stock of hard candies, chocolate bars, and lollipops. When the farmer had departed, Gedney came over to them.

"What's the big idea?" he demanded of Tim. "Thought you two were off to the movies. Run out of gas—or what?"

"Look here, Mr. Stevens," said Tim. "I told Lois about our scheme for tonight, and we decided not to go to the movies, as it might be rather late when we got back. She wants to join us watching tonight. Think it would be safe?"

Old Gedney looked rather stumped, pushed his glasses up on his forehead, and observed:

"Well, 'tain't my idee of an evening's entertainment fer yer best gal, and I ain't so sure it's any too safe either! Might be some shootin' goin' on, fer all I kin tell. Don't know as old Si'd thank me fer gittin' one of his nieces into this mess."

"Oh, Mr. Stevens, *please* let me go along!" pleaded Lois. "I'll do *exactly* what you tell me—stay put anywhere you want to place me, and I won't move from it unless you tell me to. Only I want *so* much to know what's going on! Maybe I can help you, too. I can keep my eyes open and perhaps see something you don't." She looked so appealing that Gedney could not resist her plea, though his better judgment warned him that girls had best be left out of this affair.

"All right!" he capitulated. "Mebbe ye can be of some help. We could cross the little footbridge over the crick near the house and put ye up in the first crotch of that big old willow tree jest acrost the stream from the house. Ye could keep watch from there on the front of the place whilst we scout around the back. An' every oncet in a while we'd come back ter ye and see if ye'd spied anything goin' on in your vicinity."

"We'd better take some blankets for her to wrap up in, too," chimed in Tim. "The night's fairly mild for winter, but it'll be chilly setting up there any length of time. I'll fetch along the two robes from the car. And, by the way, we'd better leave the car right here by the store. It would only rouse suspicion if we tried to go over in that."

"When do we start?" demanded Lois, all impatience for the adventure to begin.

"Can't leave till eight-thirty," said Gedney. "I close the store just about then every night, for after that everyone around here's to bed. But before that they come in to buy what they didn't git a chance to during the day. You folks can set in my room in the back, and I'll come in and talk to ye in between whiles." He opened the door into the rear apartment, lighted the lamp, brought in a supply of chocolate bars to help while away the time, and went out to tend to a customer, as the two visitors settled themselves by the big, warm range and began munching chocolate. Presently he came in during a free moment.

"I'll tell ye what's happened during the week," he said, "so's ye'll be up to date by the time we start out. I've hung around that little old dump every night, off and on, since last Saturday. Sometimes I've stayed as late as two or three in the mornin', sometimes I'd go to bed early, get a sleep, and then set up over there the rest of the night. Had my gun with me, of course, and usually I hid in the bushes not far from the house a bit down the road. One night it was pourin' rain and I spent some of that huddled up in a corner of the little porch. Figured that a rainy night would be jest the thing to 'tract anyone that had designs, 'cause they'd sure think nobody'd be around.

"Well, let me tell ye—every night but one—and that was the rainy one—*there was somethin' or somebody pokin' around that place!* Yes, sir—rustlin' around in the bushes or the edge of the woods—never come reel nigh the house—maybe sensed I was there—but, anyhow, *there was some-one!*" He looked to his listeners for appreciation, and he certainly got it.

"But didn't you even get a *sight* of him?" demanded Tim.

"Nary a sight!" declared Gedney.

"Then how did you know anyone was there?" Lois want-ed to know.

"I got ears—and they're in pretty good condition yet," chuckled Gedney. "And I kept hearin' a rustle, rustle, an' steps on the gravel sometimes, an' once a sound like some-body caught their coat or trousers on the briers an' got a good rip."

"Sure it wasn't a dog or some other animal?" questioned Tim.

"Say, didja ever hear a dog say, *'Ouch!'*? 'Cause that's what happened when the rip came. Got a good bit of some-body's skin too, I reckon!" He cackled reminiscently over this phase of the affair.

"Did they ever seem to be trying to get *into* the house?" asked Tim.

"Not while *I* was around," asserted Gedney, "and I'm pretty durned sure they wouldn't try it in the daytime, 'cause they got caught at *that* before." At that moment another customer came into the store, and Gedney had to go out and wait on him. From that time till closing, he had a steady flow of customers, and there was no more oppor-tunity for conversation in the back room. But at eight-thirty the last one had been ushered out, and Gedney locked and bolted the store door and blew out the kerosene lamps. When he came back, he said he was ready to start, and they all left by a side door that opened from his room. Tim drove his car around to the side and parked it there, so that it should arouse less notice, in the rare case that anyone they knew should happen to be about at that time of night. Then, with two car robes over Tim's arm, the three started out on their singular quest.

Gedney suggested that instead of walking along the main road and turning down the little lane beside the Coleman house, they go down the rougher lane beside his own place (which was parallel to the former), skirt the stream till they come to the foot-bridge, then cross over and establish Lois in the fork of the big tree and cross back to do their own scouting around the little brick house. It seemed like a fine idea, but was destined to have some unforeseen later complications.

The darkness of the black, moonless night was intense. Each of the three was provided with a flashlight, but they dared not use them at that time, for fear of calling attention to their progress, if anyone sufficiently interested should be about. So they stumbled along in the dark, trying to make as little sound as possible, Lois grabbing frantically at Gedney or Tim whenever her high-heeled pumps slipped over a stone or into a rut.

"Oh, if I had only known what we were going to do to-night, I'd never have worn these things!" she moaned half-laughingly to them. "But it's too late to go back and change now."

They crossed the narrow little footbridge at last, hearing the running water gurgling underneath, scrambled through the bushes a short distance on the other side, and found the huge old willow tree in which Lois was to be lodged. Stopping occasionally to listen, they saw no sign and heard no sound out of the ordinary from the other side of the stream. Tim made a step out of his clasped hands, and Lois put her foot in it and was hoisted to the low, dividing crotch of branches in the great willow tree. They tucked the blankets around her, gave her one of the flashlights and bade her stay where she was without fail, no matter what happened, and "holler like sin," as Gedney expressed it, if anything should go amiss! After that they left her, sneaking away soundlessly in the darkness. And with great inward excitement she prepared to keep her vigil.

For what seemed an interminable period, she crouched in her none too comfortable perch and listened and strained her eyes into the velvet blackness of the night. She could barely discern the faint outline of the little porch and house front across the stream, but that was all. And for a while she concentrated intensively on that. But as nothing untoward seemed to happen in relation to it, she presently found her attention drifting to other aspects of her unusual location.

Lois had never been out alone on a winter night before in the depths of the country. She soon became aware of many heretofore unrealized aspects of such a situation. Predominant among them was the rush and gurgle of the little stream, whispering and chuckling to itself in its flow. In New England, she reflected, this stream would probably have been ice-bound from December to the following April, almost without a break. Here she had not yet seen it with more than a thin film of ice that melted in one morning of strong sunlight. She became conscious that there were sounds all about, outside of that made by the stream—the groaning and creaking of bare branches swaying in the wind, little rustlings and disturbances among the bushes, as of rabbits or field mice skittering about on their mysterious errands. Once there was an agonized, tiny scream, as of a kitten or other small animal in desperate pain. It was soon silenced, and Lois, shuddering, knew it to be a half-grown rabbit, probably, caught by a weasel or some other night-prowling, four-footed marauder. Then a dog at a distant farm began to bark and bark, keeping it up endlessly and determinedly, till it too became silent, having been un-doubtedly called into the house by its exasperated owner. And after that there was a long silence.

Lois at last began to grow stiff and cramped and cold and extremely weary of the inaction. It was all so different from what she had imagined it would be when first she had started out. Where were the thrill and excitement she had expected, the breath-taking suspense? She began to grow a little irritated also, because Tim and Gedney had not ful-filled their promise to come back at intervals and let her know how things were progressing. She wondered if she dared get down from her perch and walk around a bit to limber up and get a little warmer. But considering that in the dark she might not be able to get back without assist-ance, she soon gave up that idea.

Once she covered her flashlight carefully with an end of one of the car robes and looked at the time by her wrist watch. She was astonished to find it was only a little after nine o'clock. Could it be possible that she had been in this uncomfortable nook less than an hour? How the time dragged! She moved herself noiselessly into a less cramped position and prepared to continue her vigil. The next phase was that the inaction was causing her to grow sleepy, and she began to find it difficult to keep her eyes open and watch. And presently, without her realizing it, she had dropped off into a doze.

She was roused to consciousness with a start. Something—someone—was scuttling through the bushes on her side of the stream. She could scarcely suppress a little cry of terror, as a dark figure hurtled toward her and crouched down, panting, at the foot of the very tree where she sat shuddering in the branches, scarcely seven feet above!

18. The Empty Room

SILAS TROTT had not acknowledged the fact to anyone, but for the past day or two he had been feeling, physically, better than at any other time since the beginning of his illness. He was taking more interest in his food, his limbs were stronger when he moved about, and his mind seemed to have decidedly cleared of the general apathetic attitude and lack of interest in life that had wrapped it like a smothering fog for many weeks past. Added to that, his heart had ceased to palpitate and thud with every slightest exertion, stopping his very breath with its strained thumping whenever he moved about. The discovery had come to him with almost an exhilaration of joy, and he began to think the doctor had been all wrong when he had prophesied that that heart would never feel normal again. In short, Silas told himself, he was beginning to be his old self once more!

But he realized, too, something else. He was going to have difficulty with the family if he allowed them to see him moving about too freely or returning to any of his former affairs. Ellen watched him like a cat, and the slightest symptom of unusual locomotion brought her clumping in heavily from the kitchen to remonstrate and get him back to his accustomed place in the wheel chair. He foresaw plainly that he would have to educate them very gradually into the idea that he was growing stronger and could not much longer be restrained into an invalid routine. He must be rather wily about it.

There was something that had been on his mind for quite a while that he felt he would like to attend to, and as most of the family were expecting to be out that evening, he judged that it would be a propitious time to take for the matter. So, shortly after a supper that he had thoroughly enjoyed, he gave the excuse that he was a bit tired and would go to his room rather early. Ellen had made no comment, save to present him with a glass of hot milk before he retired, and he left her washing the dishes in the kitchen and presumably talking to Zeph, though curiously enough, he heard no sound of conversation.

But in his room he did not undress and get into bed at once, as was usual. Instead he drew a comfortable chair up to the table where stood his lighted lamp, spread a warm blanket over his knees, and sat down to read till the house should be sufficiently quiet for him to pursue his plan. He well knew that Ellen would be fussing about for quite some time yet. And as she was undoubtedly planning to sit up and wait for both Jean and Lois to come in, she likely would not retire to her room as she usually did when all the family was safely in the house. Knowing her ways, he figured that she would undoubtedly settle herself in the kitchen and read or sew, and later probably fall asleep under the influence of the warmth and quiet and her own weariness. He would wait for that.

He read desultorily for a while and then dozed himself, waking to hear a clock with a cathedral chime on his mantel strike a half-hour. Glancing toward it, he found it was half-past eight. He rose and tiptoed to the door, opening it softly. The house was very still. Ellen was undoubtedly sewing or sound asleep by the kitchen fire. Just to make sure, he crept softly along the hall and peeped in through the kitchen door that was slightly ajar. Yes—just as he had suspected!— Ellen was sitting before the kitchen range, her darning dropped in her lap, her head leaning back against her chair, her eyes closed in peaceful slumber. And if he needed more assurance, there was presently wafted toward him the sound of a gentle snore!

"Now for it!" he exulted mentally, as he softly stepped back to his room to provide himself with his flashlight. With this and his reading glasses, he proceeded back along the hall, closing the kitchen door noiselessly as he passed. That would keep Ellen from hearing any sounds she was not supposed to hear!

At the foot of the stairs, he paused. The doctor had warned him specifically against climbing stairs. He was simply and unconditionally *not* to do it—at least for the present. And Silas's own common sense told him the strain the stair-climbing invariably caused a none too well-ordered heart.

"But I'll take it very, very slowly," he told himself. "One step at a time, and rest in between every one. Surely that cannot do me any harm!" He did exactly that, and in consequence reached the top with no apparent damage to himself. But the process had consumed a woeful amount of the short time he would have for his errand. Along the upper hall he quietly slipped, got out his key ring from his pocket, and, with the help of the light from the flashlight, inserted the proper key into the lock of the empty room.

When the door was opened and he had gone in, he did not close and lock it after him, as had been his procedure in the past, but left it standing slightly ajar, so that he might the better hear any sounds of interruption. This done, he

flashed the light about the room, to see if it had been in any
way disturbed during his long absence. But the closed and
shuttered windows, the bare paneled walls, the empty fireplace, and the floor with its one handsome spot of color, the
oriental rug, stood out exactly the same as they had always
been. Satisfied, he turned his light toward the wall directly
to the right of the door, searched it for some minute spot
known only to himself, pressed a finger on that spot, and
one of the white-painted wooden panels sprang a bit and
opened outward like a small door, revealing an open space
behind it, shelved like a safe or closet. Out of this recep-
tacle he drew a roll of something resembling a map, un-
rolled it, smoothed it out, and hung it on a nail in the ad-
joining panel. This done, he stood for many long moments
studying it, one hand holding the flashlight turned squarely
upon it, a finger of the other tracing certain points, and
muttering softly to himself at intervals. Once he interrupted
this pursuit to extract certain pamphlets and printed lists
from another shelf and consult them intently. Then he re-
placed them and went back to the map. He became so absorbed, at last, that he had no idea of the flight of time.

It was a long while later that he became aware, in the
subtle fashion in which such things are impressed on us,
that he was the object of intent regard from some quarter.
Well was it for Silas Trott in that moment that he possessed
not only the calm, Quaker temperament, but had also been
trained for many years past to be on his guard. Had he
swung around quickly or displayed any suspicion of an
alien presence in his vicinity, he might not have survived
the next few moments. As it was, he kept himself perfectly
immovable, merely shifting his eyes toward the door, which
was on his right, scarcely five feet away, and ajar as he had

left it. Through the crack (which was a fairly wide one) he was aware of an eye regarding him intently!

In a single flash of insight, Silas was instantly sure of one thing. That eye belonged to no member of his family—not even Zeph. To begin with, he trusted them all so implicitly that he felt them incapable of such surreptitious spying on him. In addition to that, he realized that the eye belonged to some person taller than any of them. It was on the level with his own eyes, and he was a fairly tall man. How the intruder could have entered the house, he did not stop to speculate. Someone was there—and must be dealt with. Without changing his position he quietly remarked:

"Thee might as well come in. I know that thee is there!"

An instant of absolute silence followed. It had been preceded by a slight, almost inaudible gasp. Then the door was flung open and revealed a tall, dark, handsome woman wrapped in a heavy ulster, a soft felt hat pulled down well over her face. She stood framed in the doorway, one hand grasping a handbag, the other held slightly behind her back. Silas turned and regarded her gravely. Then he spoke.

"So you are back again!" The woman flushed darkly, and her eyes narrowed.

"Yes, I'm back. You know what for! Better give me the dope this time. I happen to know you're alone in the house. Your whole family is out chasing me around the lot —even that big lummox of a cook."

Silas absorbed this information with considerable surprise, though he was careful not to show it. He merely remarked:

"You would do well to give up this useless quest. I do not happen to have what you are after—and I would not give it to you if I had."

"You know where it is, though—and that's enough for

me!" she snapped back at him. "If *he* hadn't been such a mess, I would have had it long ago!"

"It is well that he is dead," said Silas gravely. "You were always his evil genius. I think he repented in the end— though he never had the courage to declare it."

"He was an utter fool!" the woman muttered scathingly. "Hadn't the courage of a cockroach—but he knew his stuff." Her glance wandered greedily to the shelves behind the open panel. "Once for all—are you going to give me the dope?"

"No!" His reply was unemphatic but absolutely final.

"I am armed!" she retorted. "I can finish you off and clean out your shelves there and get away without a soul knowing it. But I don't want to do it unless I have to." Silas continued to regard her gravely, facing her with the flashlight in one hand.

"You may as well do so, then," he answered quietly, "for I shall never give over of my own free will!"

The woman stood watching him for a moment, immovable, wary, measuring apparently the strength of his resolve, hoping for some break in his armor of serene, imperturbable Quaker calm. Suddenly he was amazed to see her jump backward with a low, gasping cry, and turn astonished to gaze into the black hall behind her. And from the blackness issued an excited, childish treble, commanding:

"Hands up! I've got your gun—and I know how to use it, too! My daddy taught me long ago. Get out of the way, Uncle Si! I'm going to shoot if she doesn't do just what I tell her, and I don't want to hit you too!" Automatically Silas Trott stepped out of range of the doorway, but he called:

"Don't thee do any unnecessary damage, Jean. I think she will go quietly. Don't get excited!"

"You *bet* she'll go quietly!" exulted Jean. "Right down to

Gedney Stevens, too. Then he can arrest her and put her in prison!"

"*No*, Jean!" commanded Silas Trott. "I forbid that. See that she gets out of the house and let her go. She is harmless now. She will not try this again."

"Very well," agreed Jean, enormously disappointed that she was not to be allowed to follow out her spectacular plan. "Get going!" she commanded the rigid figure in the doorway, whose face, drained now of every drop of color, showed wan and frightened in the light of the flashlight. "And keep those hands up if you don't want me to pump you full of holes!"

Even in this extremity, Silas found time to wonder where Jean had ever managed to acquire this amazing slang. The woman turned and retreated from the doorway, her hands still in the air, her handbag waggling incongruously in one of them. Silas came to stand in the doorway to light the way down the dark hall and stairs. And Jean, standing in the doorway of her own room, kept the woman covered with a small, automatic revolver, held in a steady, determined right hand. Down the stairs the woman progressed, slowly, feeling her way with her feet, her hands always high above her head. Silas came to light the progress over the banisters, and Jean followed, a discreet distance behind, till at last the intruder was out on the dark porch and down the steps.

"You go *that* way!" Jean commanded, pointing down the road and out of the town by the nearest way. "And don't you come back, because I'll be waiting around here with this gun for quite some while!" She stood on the porch, with the revolver aimed, till the woman had disappeared into the darkness. And when she was presently joined by Silas, who had come slowly down the steps behind her, he bade her lower her weapon and come indoors, as there was now no further danger of the intruder's return. Still terribly overwrought with excitement, she was loath to do so, but he quietly possessed himself of the weapon, drew her in, and shut the door. And then, to the amazement of both of them, in the warm security of the living room, she suddenly dropped to the floor at his feet and burst into a wild passion of weeping. Realizing that it was only the effect of relaxation of the terrible tension she had been under, Silas let her cry it out, while he sat with her head on his knees, his hand gently stroking her tumbled hair.

Presently the spasm of weeping passed, and she grew calmer, wiping her eyes rather shamefacedly,

"I'm awfully sorry, Uncle Si!" she gulped. "I don't know *what* made me cry. I'm really very happy."

"There, there, there, my dear!" he answered. "I understand perfectly why thee did that. Thee has been a very brave girl—and I am grateful. But how does it come that the house was deserted—at this time of night?" A grandfather's clock in the corner indicated that it was well after eleven. "Where are Lois—and Ellen?"

"It's the queerest thing," said Jean, "they all seem to be messing around the little brick house—in the dark! Lois and Tim and Zeph—and someone else too. I couldn't make out who it was. And then Ellen went out there too. I think she was looking for me 'cause I didn't come in at nine as I promised. I sneaked over there instead, 'cause Zeph had told me he saw some footprints around the house late this afternoon." The whole of this was completely mystifying to Silas. But when she got to the second part of her recital he recognized more familiar ground.

"Then I got scared 'cause it was getting so late, and I thought I'd better get back before Ellen caught me. So I was sneaking down the lane at the side, when down came Ellen tramping along with a flashlight—and I knew what she was after! So I hid in the bushes till she was past, and then I streaked it for the house here. The door was unlocked, so I walked right in on tippytoes. I thought I'd get upstairs and to bed before Ellen got back—and I didn't want to wake you. But when I got to the top, I saw something queer going on in that room you always keep locked. There was a light, and the door was open, and someone was standing right in it—and I heard your voice talking. I couldn't think what was happening, so I tiptoed along the hall till I got right near—and then I saw that—that *creature* had a gun in her hand behind her back. And then I heard what she was saying to you and I made up my mind I could get that gun if I just jumped at it and grabbed it before she found out I was there. So I did. That's all!"

"She had probably been watching this house all the evening," commented Silas Trott, "and when she saw that everyone had left it but myself, she thought her opportunity had come. But what the meaning is of all this affair over at the little brick house, I cannot——"

At that moment there was a subdued commotion on the veranda. A number of footsteps could be heard ascending the steps, and Ellen's voice distractedly warning them to be quiet. Jean made a frantic gesture to Silas and whispered: "Oh—don't—don't tell them that—I *cried!*"

He did not have a chance to do more than squeeze her hand reassuringly, when the door burst open and four people erupted into the quiet room.

19. Jean Adds to the General Perplexity

EXTRACT from the diary of Lois:

"I never knew of such a mix-up as there was last night when we all got back from that expedition with Gedney Stevens! To begin with, there I was, up in that tree, and some unknown creature, panting for breath, was crouching at the bottom. I was scared to death, but I didn't even dare to 'holler like sin,' as Tim and Gedney had warned me, because whoever it was, not eight feet below me, had me completely at his (or her) mercy. Apparently no one else was anywhere about.

"I just sat there petrified, not even daring to breathe, for fear I'd be discovered. But the intruder was evidently more intent on watching what was going on across the stream than anything else, and seemed not to have even seen me. Then I suddenly realized that there was a commotion going on near the house. An electric light was being flashed at intervals, and all of a sudden there were sounds of muttering and talking. And then, all at once, I heard the figure below me almost sobbing: 'Oh, Lord, Lord! Don't let 'em git me!' and it dawned on me that that was the voice of *Zeph!* How *he'd* got mixed up in the thing, I couldn't imagine, but I leaned over and called to him, very softly:

"'Zeph! Don't be frightened. It's only I—Lois!' I thought he was going to sink into the ground from sheer terror—poor old fellow!—but presently he looked up and whispered:

"'What yo' doin' up there, Miss Lois?' I thought it best then to tell him that Tim and Gedney Stevens and I had thought there was something not quite right going on around this little house, somebody had been prowling around it for quite a while past, and we had come over to try and discover who or what it was. That they had put me up in the tree to be out of harm's way, while they went over on the other side of the stream to investigate. I also told him that Gedney had been keeping an eye on the place for several nights past. Then I asked him what *he* was doing in the vicinity.

"He told me the most astonishing tale, of how Jean (of *all* persons!) had confided to him a week ago that she'd seen some stranger prowling about the vicinity and had asked him (Zeph) to keep an eye on the place because she didn't want to alarm Uncle Si by telling him about it! Why in the world she didn't come to Tim and me with the tale, I can't imagine. But then Jean never does confide anything to me any more, probably because she thinks I'll interfere with her freedom—or something like that. Anyhow, Zeph said he'd been over here a good part of every night since and had certainly heard someone about—occasionally caught a glimpse of somebody sneaking around. He said he'd decided tonight, if he saw anything, to warn Gedney Stevens, even though Jean had made him promise not to tell a soul.

"Then suddenly the truth dawned on me and I began to giggle. It was *Gedney,* in all probability, that Zeph had been spying on, and it was *Zeph* that Gedney had discovered snooping about, and neither knew it but had been chasing each other around in the dark every night for the past week! Whether there had been anyone else—any stranger—mixed up in it too, I couldn't figure, but probably not. So I said to Zeph:

" 'For goodness' sake, Zeph, help me down out of here and we'll go right across to the others! That's only Tim and Gedney over there, and they've probably been watching *you* all this time!' He seemed reassured at that and helped me to slide down out of the tree and carried the car robes for me. We hustled back over the little footbridge and came to the front of the brick house, where we heard voices and saw lights flashing. And then, whom did we see, to our complete amazement, but Tim and Gedney standing around expostulating with *Ellen!* She had a shawl over her head and a flashlight in her hand—and *was she mad!* She was just about boiling over with indignation, looking for Jean, who had not come back from the Colemans' at nine, as she'd been told, and Ellen couldn't imagine where she was and was bursting with excitement and indignation! Why she had come over there to hunt for her, I can't quite make out yet. She said something to the effect that 'there wasn't nowheres else to look.'

"Then Tim and Gedney spied Zeph, and they got all 'het up' wondering how *he'd* got on the scene, till I explained things to them. Then we all (except Ellen!) had a good giggle over the affair and started back to the house. But the excitement wasn't all over yet!

"I was privately rather worried about what had become of Jean. But when we got back to the house, whom should we find but Uncle Si (who was supposed to have been in bed hours before!) up and dressed and talking to Jean in the living room. They both appeared to be very solemn about something, and Jean's eyes looked suspiciously red, as if she had been crying. I thought that perhaps he had had to give her a talking to for breaking her promise to Ellen and staying out so late. And I was terribly annoyed with her for getting Uncle Si upset and excited when it's so bad for him. Strangely enough, they did not appear much sur-prised to see us all come in together, though it must have seemed rather a queer performance for that time of night. Ellen began to scold Jean at once, but Uncle Si stopped her, saying:

" 'There, there, Ellen! Thee mustn't be too hard on Jean. She should have obeyed thee more carefully, but in this case she has been of quite some service to me (that is a little secret that she and I are going to keep!), so we will let it pass this time. Run along to bed now, Jean. Thee has been up far too late, as it is.' Jean traipsed off to bed, very reluctantly, and the rest of us tried to disentangle the riddle of how we all came to be milling around the little red brick house without knowing what the rest of us were after. We didn't like to do it—not knowing what effect it might have on Uncle Si—but Tim and I were forced to explain that we'd thought last Saturday, someone was prowling around the place. We didn't go into any details, fearing *those* would surely have a bad effect, but said we'd told Mr. Stevens about it and he'd been sort of keeping a watch there. We also told him about Jean and Zeph, and how we'd all been evidently chasing one another around the whole evening— everyone thinking the other fellow the intruder.

"Uncle Si thanked us all for our interest and the trouble we'd taken, and said he didn't think there was anything serious in it. Nevertheless, he would see that the place was better guarded and locked in the future. He didn't explain why he was up and around at that (for him) extraordinary time of night, nor did he say how Jean had appeared on the scene or what was the meaning of the strange, tense attitude of them both when we had first come in.

"I was going to question Jean about it when I went to bed, but she was—or pretended to be—fast asleep. And this morning she would explain nothing except that she had been out there scouting around because she thought something was going on, had spied Ellen coming down the lane, and had fled back to the house, where she had found Uncle Si up and dressed, and had to explain to him why she was prowling around at that time of night. She would not tell me why she had set Zeph to watching the little house, or what she had seen there at any time. She just shut her mouth tight in that obstinate way she has and declared, 'That's *my* secret. You didn't share *yours* with me!' I know her in those contrary moods and have long since found out that the only way to treat her is to let her severely alone.

"Ellen is dreadfully cross this morning, and Uncle Si very silent and absorbed. He has not referred again to last night's affair. I do think he seems, physically, very much better. Somehow I hadn't noticed it before. He has suddenly abandoned his wheel chair and told Zeph to take it out to the barns again. I even saw him going slowly upstairs this morning. Ellen was having a fit about it and banging things around in the kitchen. She grumbled to me that he'd be in bed again with another attack if he didn't watch out. I told her I thought it was a good sign that he was trying to get about again, but she wouldn't be appeased.

"Jean has disappeared again, probably with Sandy. It's rather lonely, and I wish Tim would hurry and get that wood-chopping for his mother done, and then we could go for a good long walk. . . ."

As is usually the case with the morning after a day or a night of great excitement, everything seems rather "stale, flat, and unprofitable." And so Jean found it. She had risen and come down to breakfast in the high hope that something very remarkable would occur—that Uncle Si would explain what all that performance with the strange woman last night was about. But nothing had happened at all. Uncle Si had not referred to the matter—had not even revealed the part that she, Jean, had played in the affair—a part of which she was justly rather proud. He had intimated, last night, it was true, that the thing was to be their secret. But then he hadn't even let her into the full understanding of it, and moreover showed no intention of doing so. Which was all most unsatisfactory. To make matters worse, he had even gone so far as to retain in his possession that fascinating automatic revolver she had snatched from the unknown intruder. She had fondly hoped she was going to be allowed to keep it, but Uncle Si had put it into his own pocket after the affair and had made no move toward allowing her even to see it again. And she knew only too well that it would be worse than useless to ask for it.

She roamed out by herself after breakfast and over to see if Sandy was better and if he could come out and help her do some work on the little shack they had built over in a far corner of Uncle Si's property, near a clump of woods. But Mrs. Coleman had met her at the door with the report that Sandy was feeling somewhat worse and she was going to keep him in bed and very quiet that day. So Jean was forced to contemplate a lonely day trying to amuse herself as best she might.

She decided finally to go to the shack by herself and spend the morning in an attempt at some interior decoration, of which she considered it greatly in need. Accordingly she picked her way through the cluttered enclosure back of the house, gathering up, en route, two or three odds and ends in the way of cast-off, rickety stools and a remarkably ugly china vase to add to her furnishings.

When she reached the rough little lean-to-edifice that she and Sandy had constructed out of some old boards and material they had found lying about in the yard, she pushed open the weather-stained and warped door at the entrance, deposited her newest finds in the most appropriate spots, and surveyed the *tout ensemble* with ill-concealed disfavor.

"It's too dark—and sort of rough inside," she meditated. "It needs something to lighten it up. A coat of yellow paint on the walls would do, but I know Uncle Si hasn't any paint—and Ellen wouldn't let me use it if he had." She continued to stare about speculatively at the tiny space— only about six feet by eight—wondering how she could manage to conceal the mottled and piebald walls of the enclosure, which had been made with boards of many and varied vicissitudes.

She finally concluded that the side walls weren't bad, as each of them consisted mainly of a battered window. And the front wall was largely occupied by the door. But the rear wall was blank, mottled in color and most unsightly. If she could conceal that by some means, and decorate the windows with some old draperies she could beg from Ellen, the place would do very well. She suddenly bethought herself that two or three strips of wall paper or even ordinary wrapping paper might do to hide the deficiencies of that back wall. She knew of no such commodity about the place, but she had twenty-five cents in her little purse, and with it she determined to go down the street to Gedney Stevens's store and see if he could sell her the wished-for covering.

Trade being always dull in the morning, Gedney was alone in the store when she entered. He was somewhat perplexed at her request, saying he didn't keep wall paper these days, as there was very little demand for it, and his stock of wrapping paper was temporarily so low that he didn't feel he should part with the quantity she would need. He advised trying some paint for her purpose (which she had had to explain to him at some length). But this she had to refuse, on the ground that Ellen had positively forbidden her to use it, she having the insurable propensity to get the main portion of it on her clothes! Gedney scratched his head and considered the situation. Jean had always been a great favorite of his, and he wanted to gratify her whim if possible. Finally he had a happy thought.

"Lookee here!" he suddenly suggested. "I think I got somethin' 'll jest fill the bill to the queen's taste! How 'bout a picture—a good big, framed picture? I got one outside in my storeroom I think'll be just the thing. Fill up nearly the whole space—don't ye know? You stay here an' mind the store whilst I git it."

"Oh, but I couldn't pay for anything so expensive as a *picture!*" Jean expostulated. But Gedney was already on his way, and Jean was left to roam around the store till his return. He presently entered from the rear, bearing awkwardly with him a large wooden-framed picture whose subject she could not see till he placed it triumphantly down in front of her.

"Now then, how's that?" he gleefully demanded. "Couldn't fill up yer wall better'n with that, could ye?" Jean looked, astounded, at the creation before her. Privately she thought she had never seen so ugly a painting. It was a marine scene, about five feet long by three high. The painting was done in crude colors, the waves, of a bright blue, as stiff and regular as if they had been executed with a curling iron. Over them sailed a ship, of no known model, while at one side a lighthouse of enormous proportions occupied an infinitesimal strip of vivid green land. The background was a sunset of intense yellows and pinks. The frame was a wooden affair of many curlicues overlaid with gilt.

"It—it's very nice, Mr. Stevens," faltered Jean, "and I think it would fit the space too. But I couldn't afford to pay for it, I'm very sure. I—I only have a quarter."

"Oh, that's all right—quite all right!" he declared. "I'm so glad ter get rid of it, I'd give it away! Ye see, I bought it once at a sale. Years ago. It was in with a lot of other things, an' I jest took it 'long with the rest. But I never had no place ter put it. Never was much on art myself—an' so it's jest been clutterin' up the storeroom all these years. Now you jest take it an' oblige me by gittin' it out o' my road!"

"But you'll have to let me give you the quarter for it then," agreed Jean. "'Cause that is something I'm *buying*—not asking for! And I can't take it unless you do."

"Very well, s'pose I'll have to if ye insist, though it's over-chargin' ye at that!" chuckled Gedney. "And jest to make the bargain even, ye'll have to cart away some of this truck too!" And he filled her sweater pocket with a number of lollipops and chocolate bars, pushing her out of the door with her load, to avoid further remonstrances about it.

"Like ter help ye home with it," he called after her, "but I jest can't leave the store alone at present. Sergei, he's gone ter Trenton today." Jean assured him that she could manage very well by herself, adjusted the big canvas to balance over her head, and so laden went staggering up the road toward her home. It was a blowy, windy winter day, and she found it no easy task to keep the thing in place, as it had a tendency to slue around at intervals like a sail. Once a sudden gust tore it completely out of her grasp and hurtled it to the side of the road, where it was stopped by a tall hedge. When she retrieved it, she found that a consid-erable two-sided slit had been torn in one corner.

When at last she staggered in through her own gate with her burden, she encountered the astonished gaze of Silas Trott, who was seated by the front window. And before she had managed to jockey her find through the gate, he had opened the door and was waiting for her on the porch.

"Whatever has thee there, Jean?" he inquired, chuckling over the discrepancy in the size of the slim young child and her awkward burden. Jean put down her outrageous work of art and gave him a short account of her purchase of it from Gedney Stevens.

"But I got it torn on the way home," she mourned, "and now it isn't going to be nearly so nice to cover that wall!"

"Bring it in here first," Silas suggested. "I have some glue and I think I can patch it up for thee." So Jean once more shouldered her burden and staggered into the house with it, depositing it on the floor of the living room in front of Silas Trott's chair.

"'Tis a rarely ugly affair, my dear!" he remarked, looking it over. "I've seldom seen a more atrocious piece of work."

"I know," Jean agreed. "It's pretty awful. Even I can see that! But it's just about the right size to cover that rear wall in our shack. And it'll be better than those old rough boards. I was thinking that sometime, if Ellen will ever let me use some paint, I could just paint it all over with a solid color, and that'll be much nicer."

"Well, now, let us see what damage thee has here," remarked Silas, adjusting his spectacles and fingering the slit down at one side. "Run into my room, Jean, and bring me that little pot of glue thee will find standing on my mantel. We can easily fix this." He had laid the crude painting face upward on the floor and was kneeling beside it. Jean ran to do his bidding and was gone some little time, as there were several jars and bottles on his mantel and she had to make sure which was the right one.

When she returned with it to the living room, she found,

to her horror and amazement, the painting still lying on the floor—and Silas Trott stretched out beside it, eyes closed, face colorless, in a state of complete unconsciousness!

20. Silas Trott Lifts the Veil

IT WAS Jean's shrill cry for help that brought the household running to the spot. In three minutes, Ellen, Lois, and Zeph had hurried into the room, and Tim, who was out in his side yard and had been called by Lois, shortly joined them. Groaning and muttering "I told him so!" Ellen had the presence of mind to rush immediately for some medicine that the doctor had left for just such an emergency, and forced some drops of it through the colorless lips, before they tried to lift him up, letting it trickle down his throat. They had been warned by the doctor to keep him lying flat, in any such occurrence, so they left him where he was on the floor for a space, till the effect of the medication could be ascertained. Tim wanted to rush off at once for the doctor, but it was a long drive, and meantime he might be needed where he was.

Kneeling about him, breathless with suspense, they had not long to wait, for presently his eyelids fluttered, his pulse became stronger, and with a shuddering sigh he opened his eyes and stared about him wonderingly. Then, apparently, real consciousness of the situation returned to him.

"Don't worry!" he muttered thickly. "I am all right now. Lois, will thee—put a cushion under my head? I'll lie here till I feel stronger. I have had a great shock—but it was a happy one!"

Lois complied with his request. And then, at a sign from her, they all left the room but Ellen, who remained to try and make him comfortable till fuller strength should return to him.

"Whatever was it that caused the trouble?" whispered Tim, as they all congregated in the kitchen. No one had been near him at that period except Jean, and she explained at some length the affair about the hideous old picture she had imported from Gedney Stevens's storeroom. "But I wasn't in the room when he fainted," she declared. "I was out in his room trying to find the glue he'd asked me for."

"I noticed the old picture lying on the floor," commented Lois. "It certainly is a horror. I can't possibly see how there was anything to excite him in *that!*"

"You notice he said he'd had a 'great shock,' but that it was a 'happy one,'" added Tim. "If that's the case we needn't worry, I think. He's still weak and easily affected by any kind of excitement, that's all. Can't imagine, though, what there could be about that old chromo to make him happy!"

Jean was privately wondering how it was that Uncle S had weathered the really intense excitement of his encounter with the unknown armed intruder the night before without turning a hair, so to speak, yet was completely bowled over by an atrociously bad picture the next morning. But the problem seemed beyond her, so she gave it up. They all stood about uneasily speculating on the affair, till Ellen came in a while later, to say that Mr. Trott had re covered sufficiently to lie on the living-room couch, and was apparently no worse for his fainting fit. She told Tim i would not be necessary to get the doctor at present, unless he showed signs later of needing medical attention. But she sent Zeph off to the nearest drugstore for a fresh supply of medicine. Then she announced that Mr. Trott had asked to have Lois, Jean, and Tim come to him in the living room, and Tim was to bring with him a hammer and chisel which he would find out in a shed that Silas used as a sort of workshop. Marveling at the singular request, Tim ran out to get them, and then the three hurried into the living room. Ellen called after them, "And don't ye all do anythin' to upset him again or I'll run ye all out by the scruff o' the neck!" It is doubtful, so intense was their excitement, if they even heard her!

They found Silas Trott lying comfortably on the couch, a happy smile in his eyes, and the dreadful picture braced up against a table, facing him, where he had asked Ellen to place it. With considerable amusement he watched their look of incredulity as they glanced at it.

"You must all think I have gone crazy!" he began with a chuckle. "And I don't know as I can blame you. However, if Tim will use a little of his carpentering skill to get that picture out of its frame, perhaps I can prove I am not so crazy as I seem! . . .

"Be very careful," he added, as Tim began on his task. "It may not seem worth it, and I do not care how thee treats the frame, but spare the canvas underneath it as much as possible." Tim said he would try, and gingerly went to work, prying the canvas, which appeared to be stretched on a wooden framework, carefully out of the gilt horror that enclosed it. They all watched with mounting excitement while the gaudy canvas gradually emerged from its equally gaudy gilt surrounding, till at last it was free. The back had been boarded across with thin strips of wood, which had had to be pried off first, and these lay about the floor at Tim's feet. He gathered them up and placed them, with the gilt frame, in a corner out of the way. Stripped of its frame, the crude picture in oils appeared more atrocious than ever, and they all wondered what was to come next.

"Now," said Silas, "this is by far the most ticklish part of the task, Tim. I want thee to extract carefully every nail or tack that holds this canvas to its wooden frame. Be sure thee does not rip or tear the material in any way. I know the picture does not seem worth this trouble, but I have my reasons."

Tim began on this new phase of the task, conscientiously coaxing up every rusted tack with as much care as though he were working with the most delicate of fabrics. Silas watched every move with intense interest, and the two girls stood by lost in wonder at the curious performance. When Tim had worked his way along nearly the whole of one side, he suddenly exclaimed:

"I say, Uncle Si! There seems to be something else underneath this upper canvas—did you know that?"

"I certainly do!" chuckled Mr. Trott. "That is why I have asked thee to be so careful. It is vitally important that what is underneath be kept absolutely intact!" From that moment there was a breathless silence in the room while the work progressed. And at last, after what seemed an interminable interval, Tim announced:

"The last tack is out, sir! What shall I do now?"

"Hand it all to me," commanded Silas Trott. "I do not trust anyone to do the final thing but myself." He sat up on the couch, and Tim brought the frame over to him, holding it gingerly so that the canvas would not be dislodged. Silas began in one corner, with the utmost care, to peel off the outer canvas which seemed to adhere somewhat in spots to

what was underneath. He had the picture turned toward
him in the process, so that his three watchers could gather
no hint of what was underneath that misleading outer covering. When it was all free, he stared long and intently at
what was underneath, and then suddenly turned it about to
face his audience.

"There," he announced quietly, "is what I have been
searching for these last twenty years!"

It was another painting! But in strange contrast to the
crude and repellent affair that had concealed it, the canvas, identical in size and extent with the other, glowed in
rich and beautifully blended colors, modified and softened
with the patina of centuries. Vibrant and exquisitely executed figures, in what appeared to be Dutch costumes, were
set against a background of some medieval town, alive
with light and action and contrasted color. The effect of
sunlight on rich garments, jewels, and quaint architecture
was marvelously portrayed. The three young people drew
in an astonished breath, and Lois quaveringly asked:

"What is it, Uncle Si? An old master, I suppose?"

"Exactly right!" he smiled. "And an exceedingly rare and
interesting one at that, with a very singular history. It is
called 'Flemish Fair' by Adriaen van Ostade, who was a pu-
pil of Frans Hals. I do not know what all its earlier vicissitudes may have been, but its later history is most curiously
mingled with my own. And if you would like me to, I can
now tell you its story. For Lois and Jean it is most essential
that they should know it, and Tim is welcome to hear it
also, if he cares to. Sit down comfortably somewhere, for
the tale is a long one."

Tim braced the newly discovered painting up against a
table where they could all look at it, and they grouped about

him as he lay back on the couch, sitting cross-legged on the floor to be nearer him and lose no syllable of what they knew would prove a vastly thrilling disclosure. Not even yet was it easy to convince themselves that the time for clearing up all mysteries had come.

"This is not an easy story to tell," began Mr. Trott. "It has some very painful aspects—ones that affect myself very vitally. But I will try to make it as clear as possible and spare myself nothing. The history of this picture, as far as I am concerned, runs back to the time when I was a young man of Philadelphia, born, brought up, and educated in that city, and then the chief partner in an extremely successful art-dealing and antique business that had been left to me by my father. My partner, whom I admitted to the business after my father's death, was an Ernest Sansome. He brought no money of his own into the partnership, and was, as I afterward discovered, very weak and easily influenced in character. But he was an excellent art critic and connoisseur of antiques, and I needed such advice in the business.

"Some time before this, while I was still a young man in college in fact, I had met and become very well acquainted with a young girl to whom I had become greatly attached, and that attachment, a little later, proved mutual. She was of a fine old Quaker family, as I was also, and, like mine, her father had always kept to the quaint old Quaker customs and traditions. He was a very wealthy man, and in his beautiful old, ancestral home near Bordentown, New Jersey, had a quite remarkable private gallery of worth-while paintings. The most famous among them was this very painting we have so rediscovered. It had been an heirloom in his family for many years back. And it had been come by in a rather singular way.

"It was not a purchase, but the gift to a great-grand-father of this same man, by Joseph Bonaparte, the ex-king of Spain, who was living at that time in exile at Borden-town, under the title of the Count de Surveilliers. You are all probably fairly well acquainted with the history of that brother of Napoleon, who escaped across the seas after the downfall of his brother and made his home for many years in a beautiful mansion that he built on Crosswicks Creek near Bordentown and called 'Point Breeze.' This mansion he had furnished in true French style and had brought with him a large collection of rare paintings and statuary to adorn it. He was genial and friendly in dis-position and made a number of staunch friends in Borden-town, among whom he was particularly attached to the ancestor of this friend of mine, whose name was Abner Snowdon.

"I cannot now go into the whole history of the affair, in fact most of its details were always a secret, but it seemed that in the years that followed their first acquaintance, Snowdon found himself in a position to be of great service to the ex-king of Spain. In one instance he was able to save Joseph Bonaparte from being cheated of a large sum of money, the story goes, and in another was even able to foil a plot against his life. At any rate, Joseph evidently felt himself under deep obligations to Abner Snowdon—so much so that before he left the country on his return to France, when the Bonapartes again came into power, he presented Snowdon with this most valuable old master, as a token of his esteem. And that is how it came into the possession of the Snowdon family.

"And now I come to the very painful part of this recital. I shall try to tell it as simply as possible. But first I must tell thee, Lois, and thee, Jean, a piece of news that will be a great surprise to both of you. The girl whom I loved so dearly, and who now returned my affection, was *your own mother,* my dears!"

The effect of this announcement on the two girls was such that they could only sit in stunned silence, staring at Silas with wide, astonished eyes. It was Lois who finally managed to stammer:

"This—is a great surprise, Uncle Si! I knew that Mother came originally from somewhere in New Jersey or Pennsylvania, and I remember hearing Daddy say that her maiden name was 'Snowdon.' But—you see—she died soon after Jean was born and—and I was only five or six years old, so I don't remember her so very well. And she didn't seem to have any relatives living, so I never knew anything much about her side of the family. But how—how did she come to marry Daddy—if you were the one she loved so much?"

"That," answered Silas Trott, "is the sorry part of my story—for *me.* Thee will hear about it now. It is all inextricably bound up with—strangely enough!—this picture before us. But in order to make thee understand the situation, I must go into another side of the matter. I had in my business dealings at that period, been fortunate enough (or so I thought then!) to acquire as a customer a foreigner, a quite famous French Count whom I shall not name, for he is dead now, and his reputation had best be left in peace. This Count, during his stay in America, had been making a collection of rare early American furniture which he was buying up as reasonably as possible and storing over here till he felt he could afford to take it back to his native land when he himself returned to it. And being rather saving and penurious in a number of ways, he did not care to pay for its rather exorbitant storage charges in Philadelphia. So he and I together hit on the scheme of finding room for it in a farmhouse in some obscure village in either Pennsylvania or New Jersey. After considerable scouting around, I discovered an old house in this very region, but quite a distance out of this town. And to that house I transferred every piece of furniture he bought, as I had happened to obtain it for him. I had hired a room in the farmhouse and told the inhabitants I wished to store some odds and ends there for a friend, not giving them any idea of its value. The Count used to come over here with me at times, strictly *incognito,* of course, to look over his treasures.

"I now return to the matter of our painting here. I had always greatly admired it, as it hung in the small private gallery of Mr. Snowdon's home. I used to come and sit hours before it, working every detail of it into my mind. Anise—your mother's name, as of course, you know—used to tease me about it sometimes, laughingly declaring that I thought more of that 'stupid old master' (so she called it!) than I did of her. There came a time later when I fear she had every cause to think so in earnest!

"It was an evil day for me when I suggested to Mr. Snowdon that he loan the precious thing to the Art Museum at Philadelphia, as it was planning to have a special exhibition of old masters, some loaned, some acquired by the Museum as its own proprety. He was a little doubtful of the wisdom of allowing it to go out of his possession. But on my guarantee that it would be most carefully guarded, and that I myself would be personally responsible, he finally agreed, and it was taken away by me and transported to the Museum galleries.

"The painting created a great sensation at the exhibition, which lasted several weeks. Perhaps it eclipsed many of the more prominent ones of Rembrandt, Hals, and Velasquez, because it was so little known and such a remarkable piece of work in itself. One day I took the Count there to see it, and he went wild over the thing. Immediately he offered to buy it to add to his own collection. But though he went higher and higher in his bids, Mr. Snowdon would have none of his offers, saying the picture had been so long in his family, and had had such an intimate history bound up with his own people, that he would never consent to part with it. And that was the end of that. The Count was very chagrined but appeared to accept his defeat in good grace.

"Then came the terrible morning, just before the exhibition was to close, when they opened the Museum to find that during the night this picture had disappeared from its place, frame and all, and had vanished completely. It was remembered that several other paintings had been removed the day before and taken to the storage room, but that had been from another gallery which was to be closed for repairs. It was not included in the exhibition. There was frantic searching everywhere for our Van Ostade painting, but it could not be found. Of course I was nearly desperate with dismay over the affair, but worse was to come.

"For when I got back to my showrooms that afternoon, after a fruitless search all through the Museum, I was confronted by police officers who announced me under arrest. It seems that during my absence a detective had searched my rooms, which were directly over my shop, and found, concealed in a closet, the pieces of the painting's frame, broken and destroyed and arranged as though ready to be burned or otherwise disposed of. The painting itself was nowhere to be found.

"It was useless for me to protest my innocence. To the

police the affair was obvious. I had cleverly removed the painting, sometime during the upset of clearing the other gallery, ripped it from its frame, broken up that frame and carried it all out concealed in something else, using my freedom of and familiarity with the Museum to get away with it.

"The rest of this nightmare I will not inflict on you. I *had* been in and out of the Museum that day, the frame had been found in my room, I had no means to prove my innocence except my word, and that, the court finally decided when the case was brought to trial, was not enough. My partner begged me to confess and restore the painting and he would do what he could to get me free of a sentence. I naturally declared I had nothing to confess. Your mother, my dears, continued to believe in my innocence to the end—bless her!—but her father was not so lenient. He felt that there were too many odds against me, though in his heart I think he found it always difficult to believe I could be capable of so great a treachery to his friendship.

"In the end, I, an innocent man, went to prison for five years and was forgotten by the world. I was thankful that I had no family to be dragged down by my unearned disgrace, and I released Anise Snowdon from her secret engagement to marry me. For a while she continued to correspond with me in the prison, protesting always her belief in my complete innocence of the crime I was charged with. But the years are long, and she saw me but seldom, and it was only natural that in the course of time she should meet someone else she could learn to care for. She finally did, and that man was your father.

"She wrote me of it in the prison, and her letter showed uncertainty as to how she should act in the matter. For I think she still felt she owed an allegiance to me. But I told her that she must by all means marry this man if she cared for him. Our romance had been killed by the cruel act of some unknown person. It must never be resurrected. I should certainly not marry her when I came out of prison and drag her name down with mine, until I had cleared myself completely of the dishonor. This might take many years after I was released, and in the end might never be accomplished. I finally persuaded her of the rightness of this course, and she married him, going away to New England to live. She never knew the agony it caused me to give her up. In the years that followed, I heard from her at rare intervals, telling of her life in Massachusetts, of the birth of her children. I think she always cherished an affection for me, for the sake of the time we were so happy together. Then, at last, I read in the papers of her death. But that was later, when the prison years were all behind me.

"During my first year in prison, my partner sold out our business and dissolved the partnership. He said it was hurting his trade to be connected with a partner in prison. I did not blame him. He removed to another city and began on his own again there. But during those long, monotonous hours I spent in that jail, I had had time to think of many things, and to do considerable speculating on my own account as to who might be responsible for what had come upon me. And it presently began to be borne in on me that no one had had so perfect an opportunity for the thing as he had had, especially in arranging the affair so that I should appear to be the thief. He had access to my rooms and could have planted that broken frame there with complete ease. Possibly he had also been responsible for getting the detective there to find it. I had never cared for or admired him overmuch, though, to do him justice, I had never thought him capable of such a piece of treachery. But he was a weak, indecisive character and could easily be influenced by those who were unscrupulous. And I happened to know that he *was* very much under the influence of a handsome but unscrupulous woman whom he afterward married.

"But I must now come to the most astonishing part of my story. It was in my fourth year in prison that I received a strange communication. It purported to come from the French Count with whom I had in the past had so many dealings. I had not known, all during my stay in jail, what had become of him, but it appeared that he had returned to France not long after my misfortune. This letter was dictated by him on his deathbed, written at his request by the priest who was ministering to him in his final illness. In it he said he wished to confess something that had been on his conscience during all the years since he left America. And then he made this astonishing statement:

"It was he who had instigated the theft of the Van Ostade masterpiece from the Museum, though he had not been instrumental in the actual removal of the painting. But he had coveted it so greatly and had talked over its possession so frequently, not only with myself but with my partner, that finally the two of them had concocted the scheme for its removal by my partner, who had then sold it to him for a price that was considerable, but far less than he would have had to pay had he been able to buy it direct from its owner. He swore, however, that he had *not* been responsible for placing the blame of it on me. That had been entirely due to a plan of my partner's, and he himself never knew of it till he read of my arrest and trial. He had sadly deplored it, but dared to do nothing about it as it would only incriminate himself.

"But now came the extraordinary part of the story. He acknowledged that he had not taken the painting with him when he left for Europe—had not dared to, lest it be discovered in transportation. In fact he had taken none of the collection of rare furniture he had made, because he feared that that too might be under suspicion, since he had been associated with me in making a collection of antiques. He had decided to leave it all where it was, for a number of years, till the excitement about the stolen painting and the memory of it had become dimmed. He had gone privately and concealed the painting among his collection where and in such a way that it might not be discovered. But how he had concealed it he never told me. The priest wrote that at this point he had become so weak, and the end was so near, that he could go into no further detail. He could only crave my forgiveness, hope that I would recover the lost masterpiece, and as a further salve to his conscience, he presented me with the collection of rare furniture we had made together. Then, having eased his soul by confession, he died.

"I was, of course, greatly excited by the letter, and felt sure my justification would then be complete and I should be released. But it was not to be. If I could have produced the painting then, it might have been possible. Unfortunately, the authorities found, when they went to the farm house to investigate the matter, that the place was empty. Two or three years before, this family had become weary of trying to make an unproductive farm pay and had decided to sell out the place and go out West. They did not really know who owned that roomful of furniture that had been left in storage. No money had been paid on it evidently since my misfortunes had begun, for the Count had no doubt feared to incriminate himself by sending money from abroad and had trusted to luck that it would remain where it was till he could get it. I was the only one who knew of it, as my partner had never been admitted to the secret, I infer, even by the Count. So these poor farmers had had an obscure auction, sold their little belongings and the collection of rare furniture with them, for they never guessed, nor, probably, did their purchasers, the real value of that stored roomful of beautiful pieces. Wherever the picture may have been concealed, it had undoubtedly gone with the rest. You can imagine my despair!

"I sent for my former partner, told him of my communication from the dying Count, and that I knew his part in the affair, which I had always suspected. I begged him to be man enough to confess that I was innocent and have me released and vindicated. But he was ever a shifty character. He denied, up hill and down dale, as they say, that he was involved in it and declared that the Count must have carried out the whole thing on his own account. But that if the authorities wouldn't believe it, that was something he could no nothing about. I had not told him of the hiding place of the antique furniture, or what had happened to it, though I did admit that the Count had never removed the picture from this country. And that was where I made a big mistake, as I was later to discover.

"I spent the rest of my term in prison and was then allowed to go my way, a disgraced and broken man. But I had, from that time, one and only one driving object in life—to recover that painting if possible and restore it to its rightful owner. I retrieved what had been left to me from the dissolution of my antique business and came over to this region. My first business was to investigate the farmhouse where the rare furniture had been stored. But it was standing idle and empty, and the room that had held the furniture contained no secret hiding place or any vestige of the painting having been concealed in the walls or flooring. I almost ripped the place to pieces in my effort to clear up that possibility.

"Then I decided to settle myself in Herbertstown, the nearest inhabited spot to that deserted farmhouse, and set myself to the task of investigating where that furniture of the Count's had been sold, and to recover the pieces if possible. It would be a long, difficult, perhaps almost impossible piece of work. For there was no telling, by that time, how far and wide those pieces had been dispersed. They were such rare pieces that a connoisseur would have known them instantly for what they were. So they might have been bought in by antique dealers, collectors, or just simple farmers who would not know their value, and they might have changed hands a dozen times in all these years. The task of rediscovering them was tremendous—and I knew it. You see that my idea was not so much to recover the furniture for its own sake, but because I felt there was a large possibility that the Count had simply rolled up the stolen canvas and concealed it somewhere in the upholstery or the inner construction of some piece of this furniture. I did not figure that he would take the method he very obviously did, to conceal it under a crude and gaudy horror, such as this was. That method was, to my mind, a bit too risky. A better picture for an outer covering might have been safer, as it would have stood less chance of being destroyed as worthless. But evidently the Count did not think so, or else, in his haste, he took the only one he could find of just the right size. We will never know just why that was.

"Thus I came to Herbertstown, where I was completely unknown, bought this house which was then for sale, and settled down to my work. I began to go to auctions, principally country ones around this district. And in order to keep in the character I had decided to maintain—of a secondhand furniture dealer—I bought up, occasionally, entire lots of auctioned goods and brought them back to store around the place and resell, if anyone cared to buy. But naturally that phase never interested me much. After a while I realized that I needed a helper, and in an obscure street in downtown Philadelphia I discovered Zeph, who has been with me ever since, always loyal and faithful and trusted. I think it has rather bewildered him at times, what I was really after in my wanderings about, collecting secondhand furniture!

"I never shall forget the thrill it gave me when I discovered the first piece of furniture that had belonged to the Count. It was an antique auction sale in Trenton. I knew it the moment I laid eyes on it—that grand old Chippendale mahogany sofa upholstered in brocade, that is now in the living room in the little brick house. It had been made in Baltimore late in the eighteenth century and had once graced a stately old home there. The bidding on it was high, but I stuck to it till it was finally knocked down to me. I had great hopes of that sofa, as it seemed the most likely article where a painting of this size might be rolled up and concealed. I got it home and examined it minutely, but was not rewarded. Nevertheless I was not discouraged and, in the years that followed, I discovered many more of the group. These I stored in that locked room upstairs, keeping an accurate record of where I had discovered every one. This record I kept concealed in a secret wall cupboard I had made behind a panel. The record was most valuable, as it gave me many clues as to where this parcel of antiques had been disposed of and hints as to where the rest might be found.

"Well, the years flew by, the Great War was over, and I was still at my task. In the depression that came soon after the war, old Mr. Snowdon lost his fortune and died a broken and disappointed man. I had never seen him since the unfortunate affair that had robbed him of his masterpiece, but had always hoped to be able to recover and restore it to him before his end. That was not to be, however, so I concentrated on it anew to be given to Anise, his daughter and your mother, if I ever should find it. Then she too died, I learned, but I kept right on with my search. It had become more definitely than ever my only object in life. I knew that she had two daughters, but I had never seen them, nor did I ever expect to, except in the remote possibility that I should rediscover the painting. In that case I intended to make a journey to the New England home and restore to you all a rightful heritage.

"Then, during this past year, in the late summer, I read in the papers of the sudden death of your father, my dears, and in his obituary it was also hinted that he had lost all of his modest fortune during this present depression. Immediately I wondered what was to become of you children, and I wrote to those in care of his estate, asking what provision was made for you. They answered that there was none, as the paternal grandparents were also dead and their estate had likewise been swallowed up in the general slump. You were then practically destitute. And at once I sent for you to come here to me, as, so I put it, I had been a friend of the family and would be delighted to provide for you all. And I think the lawyers were only too glad to be rid of the responsibility. So that is my story, and here is the long-lost painting, discovered, strangely enough, through our little Jean here, to whom it rightfully belongs in part! And so I have told you all the mystery that has so long shrouded my life!"

He lay back with a contented sigh, and for a space they all sat silent, on a long-drawn breath of released tension, spellbound by the remarkable story he had unfolded. It seemed almost too much to absorb in its entirety all at once. Presently Jean crept closer to him, snuggled her head on his shoulder, and sighed:

"Oh, I'm *awfully* glad, Uncle Si, that I happened to buy that picture of Mr. Stevens this morning! And isn't it lucky it didn't get a worse tear when it went sailing into the hedge! It might have ripped through the valuable one underneath! But, Uncle Si, there's one thing I don't understand at all. How did Mr. Stevens come to have that old thing in his storeroom? He says he bought it once among some other things at an auction. He seemed kind of ashamed of it 'cause it was so hideous, only he said he had to take it with the rest. Do you think it was the auction of that old farmhouse you spoke of where he bought it?"

"No, I'm sure of that," answered Silas Trott. "Otherwise I might have discovered it myself. But in the early stages of our acquaintance, after I first came here, I asked him, sort of casually, as I'd asked everyone else in these parts, if he'd ever bought anything at that particular auction, and he said no, he'd been too busy those days to attend it. He hadn't any helper then, and he had to stick by his store and post office pretty closely. It must have been sometime later, from some other sale, that he obtained the picture. It was so hideous, evidently, that nobody wanted it very much, and it may have been passed around from hand to hand for whatever small amount it would bring. I'll ask him sometime just where he did buy it. I should certainly never have thought of bidding in for it myself! How strange it all seems!"

But Tim now had a question to put. "If you'll pardon me, sir," he began diffidently, "I wonder if you'd mind explaining about those strange people that seem to have bothered you off and on. I think there was one of them around the little house only last week. I *know* there was some intruder in there. That's why we've been watching the place ever since."

"Oh, yes—thee is right," agreed Silas Trott. "There *is* a part of the story that I have unintentionally omitted. It has to do with that unfortunate partner of mine and the woman he afterward married. They have been hounding me now for years, not content with the damage they—or rather *he*— had already done me. I should never have allowed him to learn of my communication from the Count that put the blame on him, and also revealed to him that the picture was still concealed in this country somewhere. They must have watched my comings and goings pretty carefully after my release and removal to this place, thinking that I either had it, knew of its whereabouts, or was hunting for it myself.

"They even went so far as to hire that little red brick house at one time, under assumed names, in order to spy on me more closely. They had the audacity to come to my house very late one night and first suggest that I share my secret with them—for a large consideration—and when I refused, they even threatened me with violence. I stood my ground, however, and they finally slunk away."

"But why didn't you report them to the authorities?" demanded Tim hotly. "Such a performance is outrageous!"

"Who would have believed me, if I had?" asked Silas Trott, sadly. "I had a prison record. My name was not cleared—and they knew it. No, I was rather helpless. But I determined that they should find no more foothold in this town, so I bought the little red brick house, and later, when my collection of the Count's furniture had grown a trifle too large to be housed comfortably in that comparatively small room upstairs, I carried it over, bit by bit, to the little house and arranged it there, adding to it some rather valuable pieces I had picked up outside the collection. I kept the house shuttered and locked, wishing to give the impression that it was empty. The room upstairs I never refurnished, keeping in it only my records of the search, and that valuable oriental rug which I feared to put in the little house, lest it become damaged by dampness or moths."

At this point Lois suddenly drew a long breath and exclaimed: "At last—the mystery of the empty room is explained! We never could understand about it."

"How did thee know it was *empty?*" smiled Silas. "I thought I had kept it well and safely locked."

"We saw it the night you were taken ill—Tim and I," stammered Lois. "Ellen sent us up for your keys. We could not help but see inside as we locked the door."

"I think you both most considerate—never to have asked the reason for the strange condition," commented Mr. Trott.

"Oh, we'd never have done *that!*" went on Tim. "That was your affair. But we're still awfully puzzled to know what was happening over at that place last week." And he gave Silas Trott a full account of their strange experience in the little brick house the previous Saturday. It was during their recital that Jean bounced up, suddenly exclaiming.

"Then it was *you and Lois* who came upstairs the second time and tiptoed all around the place with matches, whispering so I couldn't hear what you said!" Tim and Lois both stared at her in complete bewilderment, and Lois demanded:

"Well, I never! What were *you* doing in that place, I'd like to know, and where *were* you anyway?" And even Silas himself looked completely nonplussed at this disclosure. Then Jean, apologizing to Mr. Trott for not telling him before, since she had wished to spare him any worry about it, gave the history of *her* adventure, much to the mystification of her listeners. When she had finished, Tim scratched his head and declared:

"Folks, this is one of the biggest mysteries of all! *Who was the first one who got in there that day, through the porch window, and what became of him afterwards?* And what is the explanation of that over-turned chair in the upper hall and the groan? This has me completely stumped."

"Let us see if we cannot work it out," offered Silas Trott. "It happens that there are a few phases of this case that I have not told you yet. For one thing, after the episode in the night that I told you of, my ex-partner and his wife did not appear again around these parts, and I heard later that he had suddenly died. Whether she ever married again or not, I do not know, but I rather think not. I recognized her description in the woman with whom Lois had the encounter one morning while I was away. She had doubtless been watching my movements, knew that I was away that day and that there were strangers in the house. She thought she could get inside and snoop around and possibly get an idea of the lay of the land. Ellen foiled that scheme, but she wasn't daunted and tried it next on the little brick house, which she must have discovered belonged now to me. Strangely enough, she must have got in there after Jean had, never suspecting there was anyone else in the house. And while Jean lay hidden under the bed, she went through the place but did not discover what she was really in search of. The crash and the groan you heard later, Lois and Tim, and the subsequent disappearance can be very easily explained, strange as it may seem to you. While she was prowling about the dark house, thinking, no doubt, that she had a free field, she suddenly heard voices conversing down on the veranda and knew that she was trapped, if anyone should see the pried-open shutter and decide to come in also. She must hide somewhere, and she happened to know the house, having stayed in it years before with her husband.

"In the upper hall, in the ceiling, there is a trapdoor to a small attic. The trapdoor is fairly well concealed, being a part of the boarding of which the ceiling is made. A stranger would not know of its existence. But she did. There is, however, no way of reaching it except by a ladder, and there was no ladder about. I had hidden that in the cellar. There was, however, a chair, standing almost directly under it. She took the chance, mounted the chair, and probably with considerable difficulty raised herself into the opening, after she had pushed back the trapdoor. But something must have gone wrong. No doubt she lost her grip temporarily, or made a miscalculation in some way, kicking over the chair in her struggle, which caused the crash you heard. Perhaps she even hurt herself badly or wrenched an arm or leg, accounting for the groan.

"But when the trapdoor was shut she had attained a hiding place which was fairly secure, as no one not knowing of its presence would think of it—as you did not! After you had gone, she probably thought it best to remain hidden awhile, lest you come back again. And later she must have been greatly mystified to hear Jean banging about when she made *her* escape! How the intruder got out, we do not know, but it was probably much later, when all the commotion had died down and before Gedney Stevens began his vigil that night. I should guess at some shutter in the rear—or maybe even the same one, before thee came back and fixed it, Tim."

"That's no doubt the way it happened," acknowledged Tim, "but there's one thing I've just remembered that shows this couldn't have been a *woman*. Because the footprint we found afterward at the back of the house was certainly a *man's!* Don't you remember, Lois?"

"Oh, I can explain *that!*" cried Jean, delightedly. "Last night, that woman who came in here was very tall. She had large feet—almost as big as a man's—and she wore a pair of what looked like men's sneakers. I noticed them especially when she was going downstairs with her hands over her head. She nearly tripped and fell twice, they were so big!" Silas Trott nodded understandingly, but the other two gaped at her with open mouths, and Lois finally blurted:

"Perhaps we oughtn't to inquire what you're talking about, Jean, as it seems to be a secret between you and Uncle Si, but something pretty queer must have happened!"

"Thee is right, Lois, it did!" declared Silas Trott. "And as there is now no necessity of keeping the secret any longer, we will tell thee all about it." And he did so, much to Jean's secret delight, for he spared no pains to give her all due credit for the remarkable way in which she had rescued him from his dangerous predicament. "That is why Jean and I looked so solemn when you all came in," he ended. "We had just been through a rather startling and dangerous performance and were still somewhat excited about it. But as things were then, I did not wish to explain about it at the time, so I suggested that we keep the affair a secret temporarily. I think the intruder will never try that trick again. In fact she will have no need. I shall take steps to assure that!"

At this moment the door opened, and Ellen's ponderous bulk appeared in the doorway. She surveyed the group accusingly and announced:

"Ye'll be tirin' Mr. Trott out with this gabbin' that's been goin' on in here, and him with the bad mornin' he's had. And lunch is ready anyhow, though I think he'd better take it lyin' down on the couch."

Under the circumstances no one knew quite how to break the tension, till Tim gayly pointed to the Van Ostade masterpiece and inquired of Ellen:

"Here's a picture we just discovered. What do you think of that, Ellen?" She surveyed it with no very great favor.

" 'Tis a dingy-lookin' affair," she vouchsafed at last. "I can't say I think much of it!" With a hysterical giggle he grasped the horror which had concealed it and held it up for her inspection.

"Well, then, what do you think of this?"

"I've seen better, and the ocean looks sort of queer, but when all's said and done, 'tis a purty sunset!" said Ellen.

21. Aftermath

EXTRACT from the diary of Lois:

"... It seems strange that nearly six months have passed since all the excitement and mystery we lived through last winter. As I read over my account of it as it happened, in this journal, it seems the most mixed-up, confused affair that ever was. That I suppose is because we were all working over the thing separately—except Tim and myself—and nobody knew what the other one was doing, or what it was all about! Even now, after it is all cleared up and settled, every once in a while some one of us thinks of some particular queer thing that happened which we still hadn't accounted for.

"For instance, only yesterday, it suddenly dawned on me that I'd never heard any explanation of why Uncle Si had acted so strangely the first day after we came here, when we were hunting in one of the storage sheds for furniture suitable for our room. I suddenly remembered how Jean had discovered an old baby grand piano and started playing on it—something—I think it was Chopin's 'Minute Waltz.' And Uncle Si suddenly looked so strange when he saw and heard it. And he refused to let Jean have the baby grand to play on but allowed us the upright piano in our room. And then, later, the baby grand disappeared completely from the storage shed. Uncle Si had said he did not care much for music, but I felt sure there must be some other reason back of that. Yesterday I was bold enough to ask him about it.

The same pained look came into his eyes, but he told me at once the reason for his curious action that first day.

"He said that my mother had been very musical and had had a quite thorough education in the art. Jean and I had no doubt inherited it. She had also been extremely fond of Chopin, and he had a very vivid memory of her playing Chopin for him as she sat at her grand piano in her beautiful home. The sight of Jean, who, he says, is very like her in every feature, playing the same music on a grand piano, was suddenly so painful that he could not bear it. He realized that if we loved music so much, we must be allowed to have a piano on which to practice, so he selected one of a different type and stipulated that we must have it in our own room. The grand piano he moved away to one of his smaller sheds that is seldom opened. I can quite appreciate how he must have felt.

"So much has changed in the eight months we have been here that I can hardly realize we once lived the very odd and peculiar life we did when we first came. Though I never thought I should, I have grown really to love Herbertstown, and I think Jean and Ellen feel the same way. Uncle Si is such a dear that he would make any place attractive. And then there are other reasons!

"Yesterday some very important matters were definitely settled, and many things are going to be quite different from now on. To begin with, there was the matter of the lost Van Ostade masterpiece, which came to light so strangely six months ago. After we had recovered from the excitement of its discovery, there came the question of what to do about it. The thing seemed all rather complicated. Uncle Si declared that since it was the stolen property of our grandfather, the painting now belonged to Jean and myself, though there might be some legal procedures to be gone through to establish our definite right to it. Then, too, there was the matter of establishing his own innocence in connection with the theft and clearing his record. And since he could now produce the painting, he thought there would be little difficulty about that.

"But another question had to be settled also—what to do with the painting, which is extremely valuable. In fact it is worth so much that if it were to be sold for a proper sum it would keep Jean and myself in comfort for years to come, as well as providing for our education and music and so on. To keep it about the house was dangerous, as it might —undoubtedly *would*—be a continuous temptation to thieves, and we should be constantly worried about it. We must either have it safely stored in some bank deposit vault where its beauty would be lost to the world, or leave it again in the care of some museum, which might still prove an unsafe proposition as it had proved before. This was in case we cared to retain it because it had been a family heir loom. If we didn't have any sentiment about that, Uncle Si thought we had better arrange to have it sold to some indi vidual or art gallery that could afford to pay what it was worth. And Jean and I straightway voted to have it sold. It meant really nothing to us, and times are so difficult now that it would be foolish to keep it when money is needed so badly. And then, too, as Uncle Si pointed out, a master piece like that should be sort of public property—at least it should be in such a place that the public can have the joy and benefit of seeing it.

"And so it has all been accomplished. After months of bargaining with various persons and galleries, it has been bought by a French family who appear to be some connec tion of the original Joseph Bonaparte. Which is really quite fitting. They are to exhibit it indefinitely, I believe, at a large art gallery in New York. And if it is ever stolen again, at least it won't be any concern of ours!

"Uncle Si is so contented and happy! And he seems very well now, too, though the doctor says he will always have to be careful about his heart. Strangely enough, he says he is going to keep right on with this old-furniture business, though he will never go at it so strenuously as before—he won't need to!—he has attained his greatest object in life. But he says he's too old to change his habits and too young yet to be idle. But, there are going to be some differences. I've persuaded him into *that!*

"Instead of the terrible clutter in and around this house, it's all going to be cleared up (how Ellen will rejoice and revel in that!) and the rooms are going to be furnished with some of the really beautiful articles he has in his stock. We will have no more exhibitions in the house itself and no-where any clutter of the horrible and useless stuff that he used to buy and dump around the place. Instead he will confine his business to a collection of really good and gen-uine pieces, and a specially fine one of old Jersey glass, which will be exhibited out in the largest shed. If he once gets the reputation for selling only these fine and genuine articles at prices not so exorbitant as those in the regular art shops, I believe he will be able to build up a very unusual business. And I'm going to help him with it. That it, when I'm not busy with my music.

"For—oh, joy!—I'm to go on with my music. I am to have a little car of my own and shall be able to drive to Philadelphia and study with the best teachers available. Uncle Si thought I ought to go to college first. But I've per-suaded him that I've had a pretty thorough education as it is, at that private school I graduated from, and would rather work at the music now than anything else. And so it is to be. I'm very happy about it.

"Jean is to go away to a fine school in the fall. She says she hates the idea, but I know that secretly she's sure she's going to have a lot of fun. Ellen weeps whenever the subject is mentioned, and is certain her 'Tiny' will never be able to manage, out of her sight, and prophesies many terrible ills that may happen to the child. But I know she'll get used to the idea after a while and will have a glorious time making a fuss over Jean when she comes home for vacations. I really think Uncle Si will feel the separation the most. He is exceedingly fond of Jean, perhaps because she so resembles Mother.

"I mustn't omit to tell about a wonderful thing Uncle Si has done for us. He did not tell us about it till yesterday. He has given Jean and me the little red brick house, with all its lovely furnishings, to be our very own. We can go over and stay in it any time we wish, practice keeping house there if we want to, and perhaps live there some time in the distant future, if we ever felt inclined to. Anyway, it's *ours* to do as we please with, and we are nearly wild with delight over it. We all went there yesterday and looked it over. Uncle Si pointed to the portrait over the mantel in the front bedroom, the beautiful girl of long ago that had so attracted me that first time I saw it. He said it was a portrait of one of Jean's and my ancestors, and used to hang in the home of my grandfather in Bordentown. He said it seemed to him that it bore a very striking resemblance to my mother. After my grandfather's death, when many of his effects were sold at auction, Uncle Si bought that portrait and hung it in the little house. I know now why something about it seemed familiar that first time I saw it. It bears a very striking resemblance to *Jean!*

"Tim is coming home this afternoon for the week end. Since he finished his post-graduate course last February and got that important position with the electrical company in Philadelphia, he hasn't been able to get home as frequently as he used to. We'll have a grand time celebrating the new turn of affairs which I haven't had any time to write him about. Tim is a dear. Sometimes I think that perhaps . . ."

At this moment Jean burst into the room where her sister was writing. The day was hot, and she was streaked with dirt and perspiration, and her middy blouse and skirt were a wreck with paint stains. A brush still moist with bright yellow paint was brandished in one hand. With the other she pushed back her tousled hair.

"Lois, Lois!" she shouted. "Do please come out right away and see the shack. Sandy and I have just finished it and it looks simply *scrumptious!* Uncle Si's given us some real nice things to put in it and helped us fix it so that the roof won't leak. We're going to have a 'tea' there this afternoon, and you've all got to come—Ellen and Mrs. Coleman and Gedney Stevens and Uncle Si and you and Tim. You've just *got* to!—Ellen's baking us a cake and we're going to serve sandwiches and cocoa, too! *Please* come right out and tell me if it looks all right. You have very good taste!" she ended beguilingly.

Lois heaved a sigh and resignedly put away her writing. She knew it was useless to resist Jean in this mood. But she remarked reprovingly:

"Ellen'll give you the dickens if she happens to see the state you're in!"

"No, she won't!" contradicted Jean. " 'Cause this is an

old blouse and skirt and she says it doesn't matter how dirty I get it. She knows I'm painting."

They proceeded out to the shack, which Lois had not seen since the improvements had been made. She found it astonishingly cozy on the inside, with pretty curtains made and donated by Ellen, a quite presentable small table and set of chairs presented by Mr. Trott, and a dainty (though not intact) china afternoon tea set that Jean had wheedled from him. Sandy himself was still busy painting the outside a dark green, relieved by bright yellow window trim. He grinned at them sheepishly as he bent to his task, a huge blob of green paint, unknown to him, ornamenting his nose. Suddenly Lois, who had been staring inside, turned and demanded:

"Jean Shelton! You are *not* going to have that hideous thing on the rear wall, are you? It spoils the whole effect! The rest is really quite pretty." She pointed to the gaudy marine scene of former startling memories which had been remounted in its frame and placed squarely across the rear wall of the shack. In its quieter surroundings it stood out with hideous distinctness. Lois had not thought of it again since that eventful day when Jean had carried it from Gedney Stevens's store. She supposed that it had been consigned to the oblivion it justly deserved.

"I certainly *am* going to have it there!" declared Jean stoutly. "It isn't valuable, but it has a thrilling history. It had the honor of concealing a masterpiece for many years. And it was *I* that really discovered it. And besides," she ended with an impish grin, "Ellen thinks it's quite a 'purty sunset'!"